GISELA TOB

GRAVE DANGER

Cover by
GINETTE BEAULIEU

Scholastic Canada Ltd.
Toronto, New York, London, Sydney, Auckland

Scholastic Canada Ltd.
123 Newkirk Road, Richmond Hill, Ontario, Canada
L4C 3G5

Scholastic Inc.
555 Broadway, New York NY 10012, USA

Scholastic Australia Pty Limited
PO Box 579, Gosford, NSW 2250, Australia

Scholastic New Zealand Limited
Private Bag 94407, Greenmount, Auckland, New Zealand

Scholastic Publications Ltd.
Villiers House, Clarendon Avenue, Leamington Spa,
Warwickshire CV32 5PR, UK

Canadian Cataloguing in Publication Data

Sherman, Gisela Tobien, 1947-
    Grave danger

ISBN 0-590-12383-1

I. Title.

PS8587.H3857G72 1997   jC813'.54   C97-930409-1
PZ7.S53Gr 1997

6 5 4 3 2 1   Printed in Canada   7 8 9/9

*To my husband, Frank,
with whom I want to dance forever*

*This book was started eleven years ago as my
project in Paul Kropp's writing course. I'd like to
thank Paul for inspiring me with his wonderful
blend of idealism and practicality,
and Sylvia McNicoll, whose friendship, support
and editorial guidance I value dearly.*

*Thank you also to
the Burlington-Oakville Writers' Group,
especially Lynda Simmons,
for their suggestions and laughter,
the Hamilton Library's Quick Facts line
for always having an answer,
Dr. Barbara McMeekin
for answering my medical questions,
my expert young readers — Emily Gray, Patrick
Hanson, my niece Heather Graham, and
especially my daughter Jainna and her friends
Erika McMeekin and Cate Kennedy —
and of course my demanding but wise editors,
Laura Peetoom and Sandra Bogart Johnston.*

CHAPTER 1

Cassie opened her window to the September chill and looked out at the pre-dawn sky. Did she have time? To the west the world slept, dark and silent. The heavens in the east were brightening. She'd have to hurry.

She closed the window and turned to pull a big yellow sweatshirt over her pyjamas and slip on her runners. She loaded the freshly charged battery into her camcorder and headed down the back stairs and out the kitchen door. Even as she ran across the slope of her back lawn, the sky turned bolder with light. Perfect.

She stopped where the lawn ended at the edge of a cliff. Far below her, the purple-blue waves of Lake Erie rolled to shore. Above them spread a band of ruddy gold. Streaks of rose, then amber, then yellow slashed through the layers of pale blue sky, but she didn't take time to admire them. She checked the settings on her camcorder. It was ready.

Panning from right to left, Cassie recorded the glorious sky and its reflection in the water as she spoke into the camera. "It is September twentieth, as the sun rises on the morning of my sixteenth birthday. I am Catherine Jane Denning, and I've chosen to mark this milestone in my life by doing something beautiful . . . and by accomplishing the first goal of my adult years."

She had always wanted to do this, get up before dawn and film the sunrise. She always planned a lot of things, but finishing them was something else. Then she'd read a magazine article titled "Twenty Things You Should Do Before You're Twenty." That had inspired her to write her own list. The next thing on it was getting her driver's licence. When you lived so far out of town, that was crucial. Then maybe she could find a part-time job more interesting than baby-sitting.

There were so many ideas. She thought of more every time she read her list. For today, she'd narrowed it down to ten. She continued speaking. "In the next few years I plan to go horseback trekking out west, dye my hair blond — silken blond — and learn to develop my own pictures. I'll improve my French and visit Paris — sip coffee at a café by the River Seine. Grow decent fingernails, read every book written by the Brontë sisters, win a trophy for something, anything."

Receive a dozen red roses anonymously. That

one was on the magazine list. What a delicious thrill that would be, Cassie thought, but dismissed it as impossible. "Who'd send roses to a skinny girl with paper-bag-brown hair and precision-ironed L.L. Bean shirts?" she had joked to her best friend Maya as they read it.

"Probably any guy who likes someone funny and bright and good-looking," Maya had answered, but Cassie laughed that off.

Now she peered through her viewfinder until slowly, up from the waters, rose a brilliant slash of orange. The sun. Its intensity made her squint. As it rapidly climbed the sky, it seemed to pulse with bright gold. Cassie knew just the music that would make a great background for this. She filmed the shimmering globe until it glowed so brightly she had to aim in another direction.

Within minutes, the spectacular sunrise faded into a regular day. Cassie turned off her camcorder and gazed out at the beautiful panorama of water and sky before her.

She felt exhilarated, glad to be alive — to stand out here and finally be sixteen. It's going to be a great year, she thought. She'd never tire of this view. Every day the waves moved differently, in various shades of blue, green or grey. Something always skimmed across them — swooping gulls, sleek sailboats, mysterious foreign freighters. The storms were the best. Great sullen clouds of purple and black could bruise and overwhelm the sky in minutes. Thunder would echo in deafening volume across the open waters, and fierce lightning explode at eye level.

She was about to leave when she spotted someone running along the beach below. Dorian. Wonderful gorgeous Dorian Gzowski probably spent some time in the dreams of every girl in Port Morden, including hers. She watched the way his long legs smoothly covered the distance.

I could dash down there and accidentally run into him, she fantasized, and we'd jog along the shore together, tell a joke or two, laugh, fall in love . . .

Yeah, as if. He'll be so impressed with my trendy just-rolled-out-of-bed hairstyle and my brother's sweatshirt that makes me look like a baggy banana. And how would I manage to think of *any* jokes in the presence of someone like Dorian Gzowski?

But I do know this . . . Quickly she started the camera again, set the zoom lens and filmed Dorian moving along the beach as if he were running toward her. He stopped and wiped his sleeve across his brow. He turned toward the lake and gazed at the last streaks of colour in the sky. A perfect profile. Then he brushed a wave of blond hair back from his face and continued running. This one won't need background music, she thought. I'll just lean back and marvel.

A loud car horn interrupted her. She glanced up to the driveway and saw her mother's white sports car backing out of the garage.

The car stopped, the window rolled open and her mother leaned out. "Cassie, come here please," she called.

Cassie turned off her camera and fitted on the lens cap.

"I'm late," her mother called. "Could you hurry."

The cap slipped to the ground. Cassie scooped it up and hurried to the car where her mother, her streaked hair curling perfectly at the shoulders of her blue blazer, waited impatiently.

"Why are you out here already?" her mother asked, then added, "Never mind. It's probably a long story and I'm off to the hospital. Accident victim coming in from the steel mill. Make sure Becky packs a decent lunch. Have a good day at school."

Before Cassie could answer, her mother closed the window and sped down the driveway.

As Cassie entered the kitchen, Rumble, their golden spaniel, greeted her, and the telephone rang. Wondering who would call so early, she answered it.

"Cassie, happy birthday." It was her mother on the car phone. "I'm sorry, I wasn't thinking before. Have a really wonderful day, dear, and we'll celebrate tonight."

"Thanks, Mother. See you later." Cassie shook her head. Once her mother's beeper went off, her mind was already at the hospital.

"And Cassie?"

"Yes."

"There's still time to plan a nice party for this weekend."

"No thanks, Mother. I've made other plans already. See you tonight." Cassie hung up. She checked the wall clock — twenty-five past seven — and rushed upstairs to shower.

She stood under the water extra long, luxuriating in the steam and the scented soap she'd bought specially for today. She wrapped a large white towel around herself and went to her room, humming happily.

It's freezing in here, she thought, and checked her window. It was still closed. Oh well, the joys of living in an ancient house. She stood at her closet door, quickly chose her favourite jeans and a beige shirt and then mulled over sweaters.

A cold draft hit her back, and she felt someone standing behind her, watching.

"Morning, Becky," she said, not bothering to turn around. "Did anyone by any chance get me that blue, red and rust plaid sweater from The Edge? I could use it now."

No one answered. Cassie turned around. "Becky?" she called. No one was there. She shivered and pulled her towel more closely around her. She checked the hall, then her sister's room. Empty.

Weird, she thought. I could swear someone was

standing behind me, staring at me. She shrugged, went back to her room to dress, then down for breakfast.

A wonderful smell met her halfway down the stairs.

"Dad!" She smiled as she entered the kitchen. "My favourite breakfast — you always remember."

"Happy birthday, Love," he said, flipping French toast and bacon onto a plate. "Am I still allowed to hug you?"

"Always," Cassie laughed. "Just don't tell any hokey stories about the day I was born."

"Deal." He sighed in an exaggerated gust and held her a moment.

"Happy sixteenth," said Becky, with the same wide smile as their father. "I can hardly wait till I'm that old." She turned to him. "Can't she open her presents now? I want her to see mine."

"It'll be too rushed before the bus comes, and your mother's not here," he replied. "She hates to miss this."

She may hate missing it, thought Cassie, but she never minds postponing it for hours.

Beside her plate she saw a long envelope and opened it. A card from her brother, one of his typical warped humour ones: *Why is a sister like a silver spandrel?* And on the inside, *They're both valuable, but who knows what they're for?* Below that he had scrawled, *Sorry to miss this special one. Celebrate and enjoy it. Love, Dan.*

7

And he'd enclosed good old cash. Great, enough to help buy that sweater, if no one had got it for her. She looked at his empty chair. Two weeks already. How long would it take till she stopped missing him?

"Oh, spit! We're gonna miss the bus," yelled Becky. She slammed her glass of juice on the table, grabbed her school bag and shoes and raced out the door.

Cassie caught up with her on the driveway. "Put your shoes on now. The driver will see us and wait. You look dorky running out here with socks and wet hair." She managed not to add a warning about catching cold. Their parents did enough of that, and Becky hated it.

Becky grinned at her sister, slid halfway into her shoes and clomped down the drive.

"And here. You forgot your lunch."

"Thanks. Are you sure you don't want a party, Cass? I'll help get everything ready."

"So you can include thirty of your closest friends too? Sorry, little sister. No go. Maya ordered tickets for the Stoan Deff concert Friday night."

"I love Stoan Deff! Can I come?"

"What are you, my shadow?"

"You're just my big ol' idol, Cassie," Becky teased with a drawl. "I want to follow you everywhere."

"Speaking of following me, did you come into my room this morning while I was dressing?"

"Why would I do that?"

"I don't know, but I felt your beady little eyes on me."

Becky shrugged and tilted her head toward their dark, sprawling house. "Look at the old place. Mother might be renovating like crazy, but it still has corners that'll never see daylight. I bet lots of things with beady little eyes are creeping around in there." She laughed, then glanced up the road. "Here's the bus."

Becky sat with her friends near the front and Cassie found a seat farther back. She gazed over at her house. Greystones was beautiful by day. After dark, though, it was the kind of place where visitors stiffened at small sounds and sudden drafts. They made nervous jokes about ghosts, then laughed just a bit too hard.

Dennings had lived there since it was built, in 1870. It had been a grand estate then, from the elegant grey mansion to the acres of green lawns rolling to the cliff's edge. From there, a stone path and beautiful rock gardens had curved down to the lake far below.

Since then most of the land had been sold and the house had been cared for both badly and well, depending on its owners. For most of her life, Cassie had lived closer to town, and been only a visitor to the old manor. When her grandparents lived there, Greystones had meant afternoons of wind and laughter on the lake and lawns. On wintry evenings, Grandpa told tales about the ancestors who had occupied these rooms before them, and Grandma was a whiz at cards and backgammon, and at listening.

Two years ago, Grandpa and then Grandma Denning had died, and Cassie's family had moved into Greystones. Her mother disliked the dark musty atmosphere and the neglected upstairs rooms. She'd called in an interior decorator and begun renovating with a vengeance — the same way she did everything else.

But Cassie loved her home just the way it was. It had weathered over a hundred years of storms and history. She had always felt safe there. Now as the bus sped away from it, she looked back. From here the house seemed so small against the immense grey sky above, and the wide cold waters of Lake Erie below it. She shivered, without knowing why.

CHAPTER 2

"Cass, I'm desperate. Can I borrow your Biology homework?" Ben Jones sat down next to her, all toothy smile, brown curly hair and pleading eyes.

"You mean copy, don't you?" Cassie grinned at him. She wanted to make him work for this.

"If Rodway catches me without it done, I lose major marks."

"How do you know I did mine?"

Ben rolled his eyes upward. "How do I know doughnuts have holes?"

"Lucky for you my Biology is better than your humour."

"Sad but true. Come on, Cass."

She handed him her work.

Ben pulled a notebook out of his gym bag, balanced their books on his knees, and began writing.

She watched him awhile, noticing how tanned his hands had become over the summer. They were travelling along the Northshore Road, which roughly followed Lake Erie's shoreline into Port Morden. As kids, Ben and Cassie had explored all the fields and ravines along this road, swiped apples from the orchards, built rafts to sail on the lake.

A few minutes later Ben wrote his last word with a flourish, looked up and smiled at her. She realized that he had begun to shave. When did that happen? she wondered. He wasn't the same old Ben anymore, and suddenly she wasn't sure how to feel about that.

Ben slapped his book shut. "Thanks," he said. "You've saved my skin."

"You can't keep this up, you know. When are you going to quit that job?"

"The pay's too good and they've promised me a job next summer. Besides — " he tried to make a joke of it " — I get all the doughnuts I can eat."

"With those hours, you won't survive till summer."

"University's less than three years away. What if I don't win a scholarship?"

Cassie nodded. Ben lived just up the road from her, at the Straker Estate, home of the richest, flashiest family in Port Morden. But he didn't share that wealth. His mother kept house for the Strakers.

"Hey, almost forgot. Happy birthday." As Ben handed her a card his hand accidentally brushed hers.

Cassie felt herself blush, and quickly looked

12

down in embarrassment. She hoped he hadn't noticed.

Ben finally broke the awkward silence. "Have you taken the white beauty out for a spin yet?"

Grateful for the lead, Cassie laughed and answered, "Over Mother's flattened body. I have to learn on the old Ford — the automatic shift is easier. Besides she'd have me so paranoid about wrecking it I'd probably total it as soon as I hit the gas."

By now the bus had reached the subdivisions at the edge of town. Several of Cassie's former neighbours from when she'd lived closer to town got on the bus. They smiled at her, said hi, and found their seats at the back of the bus where the popular group reigned — and where Dorian was already sitting. They chatted and laughed while Cassie opened Ben's card.

It was one of those zany cards — a fat bird aiming to splat on a newly washed car. Ben had written "Cassie" on the licence plate. Cassie laughed. Then she read his message inside. "Here's to years of good times ahead."

"Thanks," she said softly. Now it was Ben who looked uncomfortable.

Time to lighten this up. Cassie switched to a safe topic. "Since you're so concerned — " she tucked the card into her bag and pulled out her driver's handbook " — you can quiz me on this. I'm going for my beginner's tonight."

He fired questions at her until they reached the school, then Cassie said goodbye and headed for her locker. Maya Bhargavarti was already at the open locker next to hers. Cassie had to smile at the sight. The pile of books, binders and papers stacked on the floor reached halfway to Maya's waist. The shelf on top was jammed full with texts and notes, and one book hung suspended from the coat hook.

She watched Maya reach for something. It was a graceful movement — Maya was tall and slim, with years of ballet lessons behind her. Her rich black hair, high cheekbones and large dark brown eyes could have made her look striking, but she let her hair and her clothes hang on her a little too plainly.

Sometimes Maya would twist up her hair, take off her glasses and say to Cassie, "Should I chop this off, get one of those magazine make-overs, and knock a few quarterbacks off their feet?"

"Do you really want a lovesick quarterback hanging around?" Cassie would ask, laughing.

"I don't know. That's the trouble." And Maya would let her hair fall straight again.

Now Maya turned and smiled. "Cassie! Happy birthday." She gave Cassie a hug. "How does it feel? Did you shoot your video?"

"Great. And yes. The sunrise was extra spectacular just for me, I'm sure . . . And I got a bonus shot of Dorian jogging along the beach."

"An auspicious sign of what's to come," said Maya. She handed Cassie a tiny package wrapped in a blue silk scarf. Maya always skipped cards and wrapping paper, saying she'd rather spend the extra cash on a better gift. Cassie always wrapped Maya's presents in the comics section.

"Thank you," Cassie said, unfolding the soft cloth. It held a pair of silver earrings. She noticed the intricate design and smiled with delight. "Maya! These are gorgeous."

"Oh Cassie — is it your birthday?" a cheerful voice interrupted them. "Happy birthday."

Cassie turned to see Andrea Fairday carrying an armload of Bristol board. Her usual crowd of friends greeted Cassie too. Cassie had known most of them for years. They were always friendly, but she felt vaguely uncomfortable around them. They seemed so sure of what they wanted and how to get it, while she was still trying not to say the wrong dumb thing.

"Those are so cool." Andrea admired the earrings in Cassie's hand.

"You were out early this morning," Dorian said.

Cassie thought his smile was more wonderful than the sunrise she'd watched. Had he seen her filming him? If he had, she'd die of embarrassment. He must think she was a total geek. She prayed her face didn't look as red as it felt. "I was just trying out our new video camera," she mumbled.

"Oh," he said. Then he cocked his head. "I wondered what you were doing. I waved but you just stared at your house, then disappeared around the cedar hedge."

The cedar hedge? Cassie wondered.

"You still out jogging at the crack of dawn, Gzowski?" Dorian's friend Ted interrupted. "Normal people like to sleep till the last second, you know."

"Once my dad's up, everybody's awake. I might as well go out and run — first down the road a bit, then back along the beach. I need to get in shape for soccer." He grinned.

Then Andrea said what she'd been leading up to all along. "Say, Cassie. I'm running for vice-president of student council. Will you be on my committee? You too, Maya. We need to make tons of posters, stuff like that."

"Sure," Cassie answered. Andrea ran for something every year and Cassie liked the behind-the-scenes organizing. Maya asked who was running against them, but Cassie was thinking of something else. Something Dorian had said . . .

"Right after the election we'll have a big party at my house — victory or not," Andrea finished. She flashed a perfect smile and continued down the hall.

"Let me know when you need me," Cassie said and turned back to Maya. As she held up the earrings to see them sparkle under the lights, she saw Dorian glance back at her. He turned smoothly to talk to Ted beside him, and then Cassie realized what was bothering her.

The cedar bushes grew at the *front* of her house, and she had been in the *back* when she filmed Dorian this morning. She hadn't been in the front yard at all. So how could he have seen her there?

"Do you really like the earrings?" Maya asked.

"They're beautiful," Cassie answered. Then she shivered, just as she had when she'd felt someone behind her in her room.

CHAPTER 3

"Cassie! Hurry! We're late!" her mother called up the stairs on Sunday morning.

"Okay, okay, I'm coming," Cassie yelled back, but she sat on her bed, staring at her riding pants, too groggy to move. Why was she so tired? She'd just slept a solid eleven hours, but she felt like she'd run a marathon.

"Cassie! This is your last call. Get moving." Her mother sounded angry. Cassie struggled into her pants and walked downstairs, still too full of sleep to rush.

In the kitchen, Dr. Denning stood at the door, jingling her car keys and glaring.

"Sorry, I didn't hear my alarm," Cassie said.

"We're supposed to be there by nine-thirty."

"That's only to give the younger kids time to saddle their horses. I can saddle Seneca in five minutes, blindfolded."

"And what about your sister?"

"She can too."

"I'm twelve years old, Mother," Becky answered indignantly. Then to Cassie she said, "I've got your helmet."

"Thanks," Cassie nodded at Becky as she pulled on her riding boots. "Let's go."

"I put a banana and a bagel on the counter. Eat them in the car," said her mother.

"I'm not hungry," Cassie answered.

"Take them. It's a long morning."

"*All right*, Captain Nutrition." Cassie grabbed the food. "You'd think at sixteen I could decide if I need to eat or not."

Her mother stopped, glared at her and said, "At sixteen you can't seem to get out of bed on time."

"C'mon, I sleep in once in ten years, and now I'm irresponsible?"

"No one forced you to stay up so late last night."

"Late? What do you mean? I went to bed early."

"It was hardly what I'd call early. I heard you playing music downstairs after two."

"Not me. It must have been Becky or Dad."

"Your father was asleep beside me, and I heard Becky yell at you to be quiet. You stopped just as I was about to go down."

Cassie slid into the car. "It wasn't me. I should know if I was up listening to music or not."

"But you are late, and cranky."

"Of *course* I'm cranky. You accused me of something I didn't do. I'm sorry I slept in, but

19

I slept like a stone, all night."

"As usual, it's pointless arguing with you," her mother snapped.

They drove along the Northshore Road in stony silence. Cassie rolled down her window, hoping the fresh breeze would wake her up. Why was she so exhausted? She had been out late Friday night for the concert, and then she and Maya had stayed up talking for hours, but that never bothered her. And last night she had gone to bed early.

"Would you please shut that window. It's too drafty," her mother said.

Annoyed, Cassie rolled it up slowly.

Becky leaned forward from the back seat. "Mother, Erin and I want to stay at the farm till this afternoon. Mrs. Fairday will drive me home. Okay?"

Dr. Denning frowned. "Must you? You know how I feel about you being in the barn too long."

"Don't worry about it, Mother. I'll be fine," Becky insisted. "And I have my puffer with me." She waved it in the air.

"Don't sweep out the stalls again. And don't overdo it."

"Okay, okay," Becky muttered. "Believe it or not, I'm not trying to drop dead from an asthma attack." She sank back in her seat, but a minute later she leaned forward again. "Erin's running for student council. I'm going to help her practise her speech."

"Good for you. Her sister Andrea's running for something too, isn't she, Cassie?"

"Yes." Cassie sighed. She knew what was coming. "She's planning to be vice-president this year."

"She's a real dynamo," said Dr. Denning. "Her committee raised almost four thousand dollars for the hospital fund last year."

"I know. You've mentioned it before." Cassie didn't conceal the sarcasm in her voice.

"Are you campaigning for her again?"

"I might." She shrugged deliberately.

"You should. Get to know her better. Get involved with some of her committees. Invite them over. A sweet sixteen party would have been a perfect reason."

"Why?"

"So you could widen your circle a bit."

"My circle's wide enough."

"Two people?"

"Two really good friends. Do you have that many?"

"You needn't get nasty, Cassie. I only want what's best for you."

Cassie saw her mother grip the steering wheel tightly. She hated when they argued, but she hated being pushed into things even more. What if she had a party and it flopped? What if she waited, all dressed up, decorations and little snacks spread artfully around the room — and no one turned up? "Maybe I could decide what's best for me," she said.

"Why must you always be so stubborn?"

"I don't need to be queen of the in-crowd. I'm happy as I am."

"Are you?" Her mother stared at her in the rearview mirror as if she knew better. Cassie felt like sticking her tongue out.

"Parties are fun," Becky joined in. "All you need is some junk food and lots of decent music."

Cassie glowered at her sister. "Fun for you maybe. Kids my age expect more than a PCP party."

"What's a PCP party?" asked their mother.

"Pop, chips and parents," Becky muttered.

"Is something wrong with that?"

"Works for me." Becky shrugged, but Cassie saw the hurt in her eyes. Serves her right for butting in, she thought. Still, she felt mean and wished she hadn't said it.

They sat in sulky silence as the car turned up the drive to the stables. After chilly goodbyes, Becky and Cassie hurried to the barn. They saddled their horses without talking. When Cassie finished, she went to Becky's stall and helped her tighten the girth. "Sorry I was mean, Becky. Mother makes me so mad."

"I know. She's always on your case. But I *did* hear you last night."

"Why do you automatically assume it was me?"

"It was your music. Besides, who else could it be? There's only four of us in the house, you know."

Cassie shrugged, but the sudden image of a girl watching the house from the cedar bushes flashed through her mind.

"Maybe you were sleepwalking," said Becky.

"Come on. I've never done that."

"Doesn't mean you wouldn't ever do it. Maybe you were still hyper about the concert. I sure would have been."

"Next time you can come too," Cassie promised.

"And Erin, and Jenna?"

"Don't push it."

Becky led her horse out to the field while Cassie walked back to Seneca. She loved him for his beautiful chestnut coat and black mane and his proud way of cantering. For years now they'd ridden together every week, and he seemed to understand what she wanted even before she signalled him. She rubbed her face against his soft muzzle and wondered: Had she gone downstairs and played music in her sleep last night? But why would she do that?

She decided to skip her lesson and go for a hack across the fields. The countryside felt crisp and golden as they cantered and galloped along the trails. Her fatigue, even her annoyance with her mother, slipped away in the warm September sunshine. Life felt good. This was why she loved riding.

Tom Denning entered the barn while Cassie was soaping her saddle. She was glad it was him. She wasn't ready to make peace with her mother yet. Besides, her dad wasn't always in a hurry like her mother. She knew he worked hard, but at home in his jeans and old sweaters, with his easy smile and deep voice, he seemed content.

Becky ran in behind him. "Dad, Erin and I are staying longer. Mother said it was okay," she added. "I'll see you at supper tonight."

"I'm leaving for Sault Ste. Marie this afternoon, so I'll say goodbye to you now," he answered, walking over to her. "Do you have your puffer?"

"Da–a–d," Becky groaned. "Trust me. I'm not an idiot." She hugged him goodbye. "When will you get home?"

"Tuesday. Want a present?"

"Cash is fine, Dad. See you Tuesday. Bye, Cassie." Becky ran off to find Erin.

As they walked out to the parking lot, Cassie noticed he'd brought the old green Ford.

He grinned at her and said, "Are you in a hurry to go anywhere?"

"No. Maya's not coming over till one."

"Then you can drive us home." He handed her the car keys and headed for the passenger door.

Cassie held the keys in her hand, looked at the car and felt a thrill of power. Swinging the keys, she opened the driver's door and slid into the seat as if she'd done it for years.

Then she started to worry. So far she'd had only one lesson, in an empty parking lot. She adjusted the seat and fidgeted with the mirror. Slowly she turned the key in the ignition and stopped. She needed to gather her courage.

A minute later she glanced at her father. He sat calmly, as if he didn't mind if they never moved. She studied the rearview mirror.

"Good," he said in a low easy voice. "Now turn around and look over your shoulder. Every car has a blind spot at the side."

Cassie slowly backed up, swung the car around and headed down the driveway. She turned right, out onto the road. She was driving! This was fantastic!

Suddenly a pickup screeched around a corner toward them on the narrow country road. Cassie panicked. Was there room for both of them? Would she hit it? She glanced at her father for help. He was gazing out his window at the scenery. She slowed down and gripped the steering wheel until the truck raced past. She'd done it!

Soon she swung into the long driveway to Greystones. She parked the car and grinned at her father in triumph.

"Well done," he said. "You'll have your licence in no time."

"I see Roger's car's here," Cassie said as they walked to the kitchen door. "Which room is Mother planning to rip up now?"

"Yours, Cheeky. She's throwing out everything you own."

Cassie laughed and tossed him the car keys.

"I have to pack and get ready, Cassie, so I'll just grab lunch and run. Sorry."

"Thanks for the lesson, Dad."

"When does the Driver's Ed course begin? Thursday?"

"Yes. It was the best birthday gift you could have given me. Thanks again, Dad."

"It was your mother's idea."

"Oh."

"Don't be angry with her, Cassie. She sounds tougher when she's upset."

"Then she shouldn't expect me to be her idea of perfect all the time."

"Would it help if I told you more about her childhood and her family?"

"You mean those two dragons we visit at Christmas?"

"Cassie, they're your grandparents."

"Sorry. I know. But I miss Grandma and Grandpa Denning."

"I do too," her dad nodded. She was afraid he'd drift off into that sad empty gaze she never understood. Sometimes her father looked so vulnerable, she wanted to hug him and tell him everything was all right.

"Now give your mother a break while I'm gone," he said. "And get some sleep tonight. You must be tired."

This again? "What do you mean? I got lots of sleep last night," Cassie said.

Her father opened the kitchen door for her, then followed her in. "Your mother said you were up late, and it was at least three when I saw you."

"You saw me at three?" This was getting weird. "Where?"

"Going to your room. Rumble woke me up, and I saw you walking past in the hall."

"It must have been Becky, coming from the washroom."

"I *can* tell my two daughters apart, Cassie. It was definitely you."

Cassie was tired of arguing, but she didn't like this. Why did her family insist that she'd been wandering around the house last night?

"Don't look so upset, Cassie," her father said. "It's not important. You're old enough to stay up late on weekends. Just make sure you sleep tonight." As he left her in the kitchen he added, "I'll come and say goodbye before I leave."

Cassie poured herself a glass of milk and drank it absent-mindedly. That's twice in a week someone claims they've seen me when I wasn't there, she thought. They can't both be wrong, but . . .

She tried to recall Dorian's words last Tuesday. He said he'd jogged along the road *before* he ran on the beach, and besides, he could only have seen the cedar hedge from the road, not the beach. So at the time he passed her house before dawn, she had still been sleeping.

Did she sleepwalk *that* morning too? Wouldn't

she remember something? If she really had been outside at dawn, wouldn't her feet have been dirty or wet?

But if it wasn't *her* out by the cedar hedge, or wandering around the house at night, who was it?

CHAPTER 4

On Sunday night Cassie's brother called home. Her mother talked to him for some time, then handed Cassie the phone, her eyes glistening.

"Hi, Dan!" Cassie almost shouted into the receiver. "How's university life? How's British Columbia?"

"Exciting, amazing, beautiful. I took a kayak trip last weekend, and today I climbed Grouse Mountain, which we'll be skiing down this winter. Great dorm, great guys . . . and oh, yeah, the classes are good too. How are you? Did you get my card?"

Cassie told him about her driving and the concert. When she said goodbye five minutes later, she understood why her mother had been teary-eyed. Dan and his enthusiasm, his bikes and boats and route maps, his humour — now on the other side of the country — left a big hole in their family.

She went to the den to watch TV, but she kept

dropping off to sleep. Soon she gave up. Hoping that another early night would cure her sleepiness, she headed off to bed.

The next morning as she walked down the driveway she knew Indian summer was really over. A chill wind swirled dust and leaves and blasted through her sweater. Darn, she knew she should have worn a jacket, but she didn't want to cover the new blue, red and rust plaid sweater that she'd bought with her birthday money.

She boarded the bus alone. Becky had coughed and wheezed so much this morning, their mother had made her stay home. As Cassie headed down the aisle she was surprised to see several kids staring at her. She looked around for Ben's friendly face, but he wasn't there. When she paused at an empty seat the conversation beside her stopped dead. She sat down and tried to concentrate on a book.

It continued all day. Girls who normally didn't notice her at all peered at her from behind notebooks. A few guys looked her over and grinned. It bothered her. She was used to being anonymous.

At lunch she hurried up to Maya, "Are my jeans ripped in the back — or stained? Why's everyone suddenly looking at me?"

Maya had been cramming for a French quiz. Her dark eyes magnified by her round wire-rimmed glasses took a moment to refocus on Cassie. "Hey, go for it, girl. At least they know you're there."

Before Cassie could answer, Maya put her book down. "Sorry, Cass. That was awful of me. These verbs have me so mixed up I wouldn't notice if Dracula was sitting beside you."

"It's okay. Maybe I'm overreacting. Probably a flu bug coming on. I felt totally exhausted all weekend."

"You look all right. You had a busy weekend, you know."

Cassie knew it was more than that, but she changed the subject. "What was your conclusion on the last chemistry experiment? I'm not sure I got it right."

"That was a tough one. Let me check my book."

They compared notes, then talked about the concert till lunch was over. To Cassie's relief, things seemed normal again in the afternoon, and when no one looked at her as she got on the bus at four o'clock, she decided she'd imagined too much this morning. But then, just as she headed down the aisle, someone whistled at her and called out, "Hey, Honey. How about a dancing lesson?"

She looked his way. Was he talking to her?

A buzz-cut guy from grade twelve, Kevin-or-something, grinned at her. "I hear you're some dancer."

What a stupid comment, she thought. What's he talking about?

Someone behind her snickered. Others glanced

at her, then quickly looked the other way. Confused, Cassie stood stranded in the middle of the bus, unable to find a seat.

"Here, Cassie. Better sit by me." Ben pushed his gym bag onto the floor.

Cassie sat down and started to thank him. He nodded and continued reading his book. She noticed the title: *The Seven Habits of Highly Effective People*. Give me a break, she thought. Sometimes I think Ben would get along perfectly with my mother.

When it didn't annoy her, though, she admired Ben's ambition. She understood it too. It couldn't be easy living with the Strakers, seeing what Roderick and Julia got, and knowing you'd never be able to afford it. "Hey, Roderick doesn't have half your brains . . . and you're prettier than Julia," she used to kid him.

But right now she wasn't in a kidding mood. She stared restlessly out the bus window and thought about what Kevin had said to her. Dancing? What did he mean? Why were people staring at her? For once she was glad Becky wasn't on the bus. Cassie hoped Dorian wasn't watching either, but she didn't have the courage to turn around and look.

Ben dog-eared his page and slapped the book shut.

"Remind me never to lend you a book," Cassie said, glad for the distraction.

"Too late. I have two of yours at home already."

"That makes us even. I've got a bunch of your CDs."

"So that's what you've been dancing to."

"Hardly. What's Kevin talking about anyway? I dance like a kangaroo."

"I know."

"Thanks."

"My poor toes have never forgotten grade-eight square dancing classes with you." Ben rubbed his foot.

"You made me lose my step," Cassie accused, laughing.

"Only when you crossed your eyes and made faces at me."

Cassie turned serious. "Meanwhile, these guys know something we don't." Ben nodded. "So how do I find out what's going on?"

"Don't worry. How bad can gossip about you be? By tomorrow no one will remember."

Cassie relaxed. Ben always had a way of making her feel better. There wasn't much point in talking about it anymore, so she gazed out the window again. They were passing the cemetery, an ancient and tranquil corner sheltered by trees, overlooking the lake. Usually she loved its peacefulness, and she often walked Rumble there. Today it seemed dismal. In the overcast light, its shadows were deep. A wind from the lake ripped the yellow dying leaves from the trees, blew them into dusty swirls, then dropped them, still, beside granite gravestones. Cassie shivered and crossed her arms.

The bus reached her driveway. With a short punch on Ben's shoulder, she got off the bus fast and walked up the drive without looking back. It felt better than usual to come home to Greystones.

Becky opened the kitchen door for her, coughing. Cassie glanced down to make sure she was wearing slippers.

"Hi, Becky. You look better than you sound. Is Mother bringing home supper or are we in charge?" She reached down to pat Rumble.

"She said not to worry about it. You've had a couple of phone calls. Someone is really anxious to get you."

As if on cue, the phone rang. Becky looked at her oddly, and left the room when Cassie picked up the receiver.

The caller smacked gum as he talked. "Hi. Betcha didn't think I'd call so soon."

"Who's this?"

"Hey. I'm real hurt. You've forgotten me already?"

Cassie didn't recognize the voice. Was this some joke? The speaker sighed loudly. Cassie imagined foul breath blasting through the line at her. "You've got the wrong num— "

"Don't play games with me, Catherine."

"What?"

"You danced with me on Saturday night. And you put a piece of paper in my pocket. It's got your address on it — Greystone Manor. And your name — Catherine Denning."

"I said, you have the wrong number!" Cassie slammed the receiver down hard.

CHAPTER 5

Cassie sat at the kitchen table, shaking.

Becky came in, poured herself a mug of chocolate milk and heated it in the microwave. "So who was the Prince Charming on the phone?"

Cassie shook her head. "Some nut. I hung up."

"What, you turned down a wonderful . . . " Becky started, until she saw Cassie's pale face. Silently she handed the steaming mug to her sister. "Has he bothered you before?"

Cassie took a sip of the hot chocolate. The warmth sliding down her throat made her feel better. "No, never, thank goodness. His voice didn't even sound familiar."

"Then it must have been a wrong number."

Cassie didn't know why, but she didn't tell Becky that this wrong number knew her name and address. Was this connected to the weird treatment she'd received at school today? It was too much to be a coincidence.

Cassie switched to something more cheerful. "Your homework's on the counter, Becky. Erin says hi, and Jenna and Emily want you to phone them."

Rumble barked and raced to the door as Dr. Denning rushed in. While they prepared and ate dinner, chatting, Cassie tried to stop worrying about what had happened during the day and who had given her name and address to some creep Saturday night.

Finally she went upstairs and shut her door behind her. She turned on her radio and flopped down onto her overstuffed rocking chair. Relax, she told herself, it'll all make sense tomorrow.

In her room, her refuge, Cassie always felt better. She had chosen her favourite colour — a cool soothing blue — for the walls, and a deep yellow rug to warm the polished wood floor. Everything else in here — the dresser, desk, the rocking chair, her lace comforter — was a soft ivory colour. Lace curtains let in the sunlight and a view of the lake. Her walls were decorated with posters of Stoan Deff and other rock stars, and several enlarged photos of Seneca, the fields and the lake. She'd photographed and framed them herself. Everything here was clean, comfortable, organized to suit her.

She reached over, dialled Maya's number, and told her about the phone call.

"Some no-life is playing a joke on you," Maya suggested.

"No, he sounded hurt that I didn't 'remember'

him. Maya, he talked about dancing on Saturday night. On the bus home, Kevin said something about me dancing. There must be a connection."

"But you were home Saturday."

"Not only home, but wandering around most of the night, according to my family."

"What do you mean?"

"They claim I was downstairs playing music after two."

"That doesn't sound like you."

"Tell that to my parents."

"Why don't you phone Kevin and ask him what he meant?"

"He was so awful, I wouldn't give him the satisfaction."

"I wonder if someone in town just looks like you. I'm sure it'll all straighten out soon," Maya tried to comfort Cassie. "Look, I hate to leave you hanging, but my history essay is due in the morning."

"Okay, talk to you tomorrow." Cassie hung up and tried to do her homework but couldn't concentrate. Even if her double had been dancing up a storm in town, she couldn't be wandering around Greystones during the night. It just didn't make sense. Too tired to think anymore, Cassie gave up, packed her books for tomorrow into her bag, and went to bed.

During the night, she woke up shivering with cold. As she groped for her covers she had a strange feeling someone was in her room. "Becky?" she whispered. "Are you all right?"

No one answered.

Cassie lay still, listening, trying to see into the dark silent corners. She felt just as she had the morning of her birthday — cold, watched and vulnerable. Who was there? A burglar? What did he want?

Her throat felt dry. She could barely breathe. Thoughts and fears flashed through her mind. She knew she shouldn't have spoken and let him know she was awake. Would he hurt her? Should she run? But she'd never make it to the door.

She braced herself and tried to see if anything was coming at her in the dark. She saw nothing. She lay quiet, trying to hear — a movement, breathing — above the pounding of her heart. She heard nothing. But did she smell something? Roses? No, it didn't make sense. All she knew was that someone was there. Could it be the obnoxious guy on the phone? She strained to listen. If someone was there, he'd move sooner or later. Why did Dad have to be away tonight?

For an endless, terrifying time Cassie lay waiting. But nothing happened. Had she imagined it? Was she just spooked because of today?

She couldn't stand it any longer. She had to know. She shaded her eyes and turned on her lamp. It was a mistake. The light blinded her.

As her eyes adjusted she scanned her room. Everything looked normal. But her heart was still hammering and her skin prickled. Finally she felt strong enough to get up and search the closet.

No one.

She checked under the bed.

Nothing.

She went back to bed, but could not face the dark again. Leaving the light on, she curled up under an extra blanket, and eventually drifted into restless sleep.

The next morning she found she had overslept again. With just twenty minutes to wash, dress and make it to the bus, she jumped out of bed, dashed across the room, and went sprawling onto the floor.

She sat up and rubbed her ankle. She had slid on something. Strange — one of her CDs lay in front of her. But what was it doing on the floor?

Well, no time to worry about it. She was late. Even though her ankle hurt, she ran to the bathroom. Becky obviously had not been in here; she must be staying home again. Cassie washed quickly, dressed, grabbed her bag and hurried downstairs.

"You're late again." Her mother was rushing around cleaning up, packing her briefcase and writing notes.

"Sorry, I had a bad night."

"Are you all right?"

"Sure." Cassie hurried to the door.

"Have you seen my purse? Mrs. Sheldrick will be here to clean any minute. I have an eight-forty meeting. There's an apple muffin for you on the counter."

"Try the front hall."

Dr. Denning quickly hugged Cassie goodbye and rushed out to the hall.

Cassie headed out the door and was halfway down the driveway when the bus arrived. This was what she had feared. She could have died of embarrassment as she limped to the road, knowing that everyone on the bus was watching her.

She boarded the bus awkwardly and dived for the first seat. For the entire trip she sat stone-faced, ignoring everyone, staring out the front window.

She arrived at school determined to find out why everyone had acted so odd yesterday. At least one weird thing happening to her lately would be explained. She planned to corner someone — anyone — who could tell her what she was supposed to have done on Saturday night.

A girl dressed totally in black was walking ahead of her. Cassie could tell by the girl's latest shade of sculptured red hair that it must be Sarah Lippendale. Sarah always knew the latest gossip.

"Sarah — " Cassie began.

But Sarah saved her the trouble of asking. "Have fun Saturday night, Cassie?"

"I'd love to know."

"It's no secret. The whole school's talking about it. I hear you've become some dancer."

"Oh, really. And where did I dance so well?"

"You know you can't deny it, Cassie. You were seen."

"Oh?"

"Mark Murdoch and his friends saw you at the dance at St. Mary's. You were wearing a short red dress — very short — and bugging every guy near you to dance."

Cassie was stunned. Although Sarah loved to pass on gossip, she wasn't known to lie. Cassie knew she was blushing — probably looking guilty — and hated herself for it.

"Sarah, phony rumours are way beneath you," was the best she could answer.

"I didn't make this up. I heard it."

"It's not true. I was home Saturday. In my room. Sleeping. Mark and the boys must have got hold of a bottle."

"They said it looked like *you* had. That you danced like a wild woman."

"It must have been someone else. Not me."

"I'm only saying what I've heard all over the school."

Cassie tried to freeze Sarah with a regal stare. That only works in books, she decided, as she watched Sarah hurry away to join a group of girls, her mouth already going into action.

And even if Sarah had believed her, there was still the note. Had some girl not only begged guys to dance with her, but also slipped Cassie's address and number into their pockets? Why? Cassie's ankle throbbed as she climbed the stairs to Geography class.

Halfway through Geography, Mark Murdoch stood in front of the room giving a presentation. Cassie's thoughts drifted as he went on and on. " . . . so the food problems of desert lands would be solved with the use of hydrophonic agriculture — "

"It's hydro-PON-ics," Cassie snapped. "Can't you at least say it right?"

Everyone turned toward her. She was even more surprised than they were that her words had slipped out like that. It was the break the class needed, and everyone laughed.

As they quieted down again, Ben muttered, "I guess those little *Chickadee* magazines don't come with pronunciation guides."

That set them off again.

Mark glared ice-picks at Cassie. She smiled back at him. He deserved this.

Then Mark spoke out. "I'm impressed — she's clever, as well as one amazing dancer." He smirked and sat down.

Cassie wished she had a biting remark to squash Mark, to make these silent staring faces laugh at *him* again. She wondered why it was so easy for her to be witty with her friends or family at home, but impossible before an audience like this. She just wasn't any good at showdowns. Instead she retreated, red-faced, into her notebook. She didn't look up again until the bell rang, and hated herself for being such a wimp.

At lunch, Cassie met Maya at her open locker.

As soon as she saw Cassie, Maya started talking. "You were right. There's a rumour going around about you. It's so stupid. You'll never guess what you were doing Saturday night."

"Sarah told me. Where'd you hear it?"

They discussed the story on the way to the cafeteria. Maya couldn't come up with any reasonable explanations either. "I can't even think of anyone in town who looks like — " She stopped talking to watch Cassie's awkward walk. "Hey, are you limping? What happened?"

"I slept in this morning, ran to my closet, slipped on a CD, and twisted my ankle."

"A CD on your floor? You must be frazzled. You never leave anything out of place in your room."

Cassie made a face at her. "So I like being organized . . . But you know, you're right. I was so tired and rushed this morning, that I just . . . " Cassie stopped. She thought for a moment, then went on. "Maya, I *know* that CD was in its case on the shelf last night. I remember putting it away. But there's more . . . "

With a crowd of others they entered the cafeteria, but chose a table by themselves. While Cassie tried to find the right words, Maya waited.

Cassie continued softly, "I woke up during the

night. It was really cold . . . and spooky. I thought someone was in my room."

Maya shivered. "In your room! You must have been terrified!"

"I was. And I was so sure someone was there, I turned on my light to check." She stopped again.

"And?"

"That's all. No one was there. But it felt like someone was watching me . . . someone who didn't like me."

"How could anyone not like — " Maya tilted her head. "Cassie, have you had a fight with your mother again?"

"Don't just put this down as my 'mother-always-criticizes-me complex,' Maya. This is different." Cassie was exasperated. "How did my CD get onto the floor in the middle of the night? How did some creepy guy at a St. Mary's dance get my name and address? Why does the whole school suddenly think I'm a dancing maniac?" She took a deep breath. "What's going on?"

CHAPTER 6

Classes ended an hour early Tuesday afternoon for a soccer game and Cassie wandered over to the crowd lining the field. She used to love watching her brother Dan play, and wished he were here now. This was an important game for Lakeside High. Today's opposing team was the toughest in the league, so the tension was high. She saw Ben on the bench, obviously steaming to get out onto the field. She stopped awhile beside a group of girls.

"He's so hot. I just love looking at him."

"He smiled at me in the hall yesterday."

They were gushing over Dorian, a popular pastime among the girls at school. Cassie couldn't disagree — he looked good out there — but she got tired of hearing it. It occurred to her that Dorian might hate it too.

"Are you really going out with him Friday, Shauna?"

"Yes, finally." Shauna flicked back her hair. She had bagged first prize, and was smiling as if she had built him herself.

"You are sooo lucky. Every girl in school will envy you."

"I know."

At that moment Dorian scored the first goal. The crowd went crazy, and the girls beside Cassie squealed and jumped as if a hose had been turned on them.

Cassie moved on, and nearly bumped into Maya, frantically snapping pictures of the game while trying to write on a yellow scratch pad.

"I don't know if I just photographed that goal, the sky, or the left ear of the guy in front of me," she moaned.

"Let me take the pictures. You stick to the writing."

Maya gratefully handed over the camera, and for the rest of the game Cassie was glad to concentrate on correct focus and angles, rather than her problems.

But later, on the bus, she felt snarly again. She'd stood too long at the soccer field and her ankle ached. And she was dead tired, thanks to last night's incident. Now she sat scrunched up in the corner of her seat and glared out the window. Ben sat beside her, looking as grumpy as she did.

For awhile he said nothing, but when she didn't even try to get a conversation going, he snapped at her, "What crawled up your shorts?"

"And yours too. You don't even have an excuse — your team won, and you got an assist."

"Sure, but Gzowski scored it. Why is he always the striker and I'm just the defence?"

This wasn't like Ben. Cassie raised her eyebrows.

"Sorry, bad day," he said. "Sometimes it bugs me how he'll easily end up a hotshot surgeon like his dad . . . and every girl in school lights up when he walks by."

"I don't." She hoped she didn't.

"You don't count."

"Oh, thanks. Make my day some more."

"I didn't mean it like that. I uh . . . um . . . I'd hate it if you did." He lifted his book to hide his blush.

Cassie felt flustered too, so she pretended to look for something in her backpack. There was Becky's pink loose-leaf, with the large loopy script and neat margins. Becky's middle school was across the street from Lakeside High, so Cassie could easily pick up her sister's assignments. She couldn't help smiling at the corny jokes decorating Becky's book. *In case of fire, throw this in. Fail now, avoid the June rush.* Tucked into the binder was her basketball schedule. Cassie remembered how long Becky had argued until their parents allowed her to join the team. She worked hard not to let her asthma interfere with her life and her friendships. She refused to let her parents overprotect her, and just hated staying home like this.

Cassie smiled as she thought of her sister — funny and sophisticated one minute, really annoying the next. She could also fling out some choice vocabulary. But at times like yesterday, she'd hand over her own hot chocolate to make Cassie feel better. Sometimes Becky would come to her room at night and the two of them would sit on Cassie's bed together, watching the moon shimmer a silver path across the lake, listening to the soft lapping of the waves on the beach below, and talk for hours.

A jab in the arm startled Cassie alert again.

"Hey, wake up. Here's your driveway."

Cassie said goodbye to Ben, tried to hurry off the bus, and dropped all her books. Totally embarrassed, she collected the mess and watched her pen roll all the way to the back and stop near Dorian's seat. Goodbye, old pen, she decided. You're on your own. With as much dignity as her limp allowed, she stepped off the bus and up the drive to Greystones, towering dark and imposing above her.

As soon as Cassie entered the front hall, Becky rushed down the stairs, flushed and excited.

Cassie almost panicked. Oh no, not another phone call. "I've been waiting and waiting for you to get home. Come up to the attic and see what I've found!"

"The attic? Are you crazy? Becky, with all that dust up there it's the last place — "

But Becky ignored her and pulled her along, chattering all the way up the stairs, down the hall, through a narrow door, and up steep wooden steps. "... boring afternoon ... Mrs. Sheldrick vacuuming everywhere ... explored upstairs ... tons of old stuff ... you should see ... "

They reached the attic. Cassie made herself relax and look around. She hadn't been up here for years. Two small windows draped with spider webs and dead flies allowed in enough light to see the dusty, crowded room. Generations of worn furniture, books and magazines yellow and brittle with age, forgotten racquets, harnesses and trunks were stacked all over. Here and there lay evidence of long-ago attempts to tidy and organize a section, but even those efforts were now covered with a thin grey layer of dust.

Becky led the way into a smaller area set apart from the main attic because it was under another gable. It was much lighter in here. The window was larger and less dusty. Neatly lined against one wall stood many boxes and a large wooden wardrobe with intricate vines and roses carved into the double doors.

Cassie opened it. Ignoring the musty smell, Becky grinned and reached in to sort through the collection of toys, dolls and boxes on the bottom shelf.

"Look at this." Becky held up a small jewellery box filled with necklaces, a charm bracelet, and a beautiful locket of dull gold.

Cassie noticed the initials etched into the front: DJD. She didn't recognize the initials, but she did the tiny photo inside. The hair looked dark and was styled differently, but she knew those two smiles. It was their grandparents, younger than she had known them. She gazed at them a moment, and slipped the locket into her pocket. It was too special to abandon up here.

They opened a small record case full of old-fashioned 45s. Elvis, Pat Boone, The Four Lads, Peggy Lee — Fifties music. Cassie closed the case and sat on her heels, wondering. It was all too completely, too carefully packed away. And who was DJD? Where was she now?

Becky grabbed a long plaid skirt from its hanger and put it on over her shorts, along with a pink sweater Cassie unfolded and handed to her.

Becky twirled around. "How do I look?" Her shining grey eyes told what the answer should be.

"Real cool, man, or the bee's knees, or whatever they said in those days," laughed Cassie.

"Decent! Pull my hair into a ponytail, Cass. Hand me that scarf. Oh, look at these shoes. They fit. Don't I look great? I could wear this for Halloween. Get the — "

"Hold still. Let me get your hair done. There." Cassie pulled an elastic into place. "You look great, Becky."

Outside, they heard the scrunch of gravel in the

driveway. Becky peeked through the dusty window. "Hey, Dad's home from the Soo. Listen, Cassie, Dad was a teenager then, wasn't he? He'll love this outfit. Let's surprise him."

They closed the wardrobe doors and threaded their way through the attic back to the creaky staircase.

"Slow down, Becky. My ankle's sore."

"Come on. He'll be almost up the walk."

By the time they hurried along the upstairs hall, Tom Denning had entered the front hall. Becky posed in full Fifties splendour at the top step. Her father's back was turned to them as he shut the door.

Regally, Becky descended the stairs. In a voice that was supposed to sound throaty, she said, "Hello, Tom. I've been waiting for you."

He spun around. As he stared at the figure coming down the stairs toward him his face bleached of all colour.

"Diana?" he gasped. He dropped his suitcase, took a step toward her, then grabbed his chest and leaned hard against the bannister.

CHAPTER 7

Cassie rushed down the stairs to her father. Certain that he was having a heart attack, she made him sit on the steps. He protested he was fine, but he looked too pale and disoriented, and she knew denial was one of the symptoms.

Forcing herself to stay calm, she tried to think of what to do. Keep him warm? She ran to fetch a blanket from the den. She sent Becky to call 9–1–1.

Cassie hurried back with the blanket, hoping her father would be standing up, smiling, telling them it was a joke. He wasn't. Instead he sat still, staring somewhere far away from them. She draped the blanket around him, asked if he wanted a glass of water, and looked up to see Becky in the hall, barely fighting back tears. Her father's pulse and breathing were all right, so she went to comfort Becky.

Rumble, sensing something was wrong, dashed from one to the other, jumping, licking and barking loudly.

In the middle of the chaos Dr. Denning came in the front door. With one look at her husband she took over. She pushed the dog out the door, sent the girls for water, and rushed to their father.

Cassie watched them a moment, glad that her mother was looking after him, yet angry that she had taken such abrupt charge, as if Cassie hadn't coped at all. "9–1–1 is on its way," she said, proud to show that she had thought of it.

"Cancel it quickly, before they waste their time," ordered her mother.

Cassie stomped to the telephone, made the call, then followed Becky into the hall. They were in time to see her parents walk to her father's study. Her mother took the water from Becky and shut the door behind them.

For twenty long minutes they stayed in the study while the girls sat in the kitchen, waiting. They looked at each other in disbelief. How had their joke turned out so badly?

"It's all my fault," whispered Becky. "I shouldn't have surprised him like that."

Cassie tried to set Becky's mind at ease, but she kept wondering why the sight of Becky had shocked her father so badly. Diana, he'd whispered. Who was that?

Finally, their mother came out. In her crisp professional manner she told them, "Dad is all right. It's not your fault. Take those clothes back up to the wardrobe, and I'll get dinner ready."

Cassie stared at her. Her mother knew exactly where those clothes had come from. She knew what had upset their father. She knew, and she wouldn't tell them a thing. Cassie saw her own frustration mirrored in her sister's face. Why couldn't their mother see it too?

Becky tore the offending clothes off, and Cassie walked up to the attic with her. She folded the skirt and sweater and put them back on the shelf beside the jewellery box and all the other perfectly ordered items. Then she reached into her pocket and clasped the locket she'd put there. She thought of her grandparents and wished they were here to help her now.

The next evening Cassie walked alone along the beach. Rumble ran close by, stopping to sniff something here, racing along the shore there. She ignored him and the rose and purple splendour of the sky over the lake, and tried to make sense of the night before. She couldn't forget the sight of her father — normally so strong, calm and in control — leaning weakly on the bannister, as pale as death. What had happened to her safe and carefree life?

She thought about the sad affair dinner — canned soup and sandwiches — had been last night. Dad had remained in his study. The rest of them had eaten in tense silence, a wall of unanswered questions between them, Dan's old chair seeming emptier than ever. Cassie's throat had felt too dry, her stomach too tight, to eat. She had left the table and spent the rest of the evening in her room.

She clenched her hands inside her jacket and kicked a stone fiercely across the sand, as if *it* refused to give her the answers. But it was her parents who had shut her out. Last night they should have talked about what had happened. Instead, her father withdrew, and her mother had barged in and barked orders as if Cassie had been an incompetent idiot.

She kicked the stone hard into the lake. Rumble chased it in, splashing, barking and wagging his tail, but it made no difference to the waves swelling forever to the shore.

Now it was getting dark. Cassie turned back toward home. The old wooden stairs leading from the beach up to her house were tricky enough to climb even in daylight. The only other way to get from the beach up to the Northshore Road was now behind her, just past the cemetery, where the cliff gradually sank level with the beach. Cassie sometimes chose the roundabout Northshore route home, but tonight the loneliness of the beach suited her mood. She didn't see the other figure walking in the same direction behind her.

Ahead of her the cliff jutted out, forcing anyone walking that way to navigate rocks and pools of water. Tucked into the curve made by the cliff, almost hidden by vines and bushes, leaned an ancient rickety boathouse. Long ago, Cassie had gone in there looking for an extra paddle. The silent, dust-shrouded shapes of boats and buckets in the murky gloom had made her uneasy. She'd pulled a tackle box aside. Something slimy had slithered away, and a large cloud of dust and dead insects had lifted and blown at her, and she'd fled.

Nearing the wooden stairs, she thought again about last night. As she had been preparing for bed, her mother had come in and called Becky to join them. She'd cleared her throat nervously. "Girls, you're wondering about your dad, of course. He was surprised to see Becky in those clothes." She had stopped for a deep breath. "You know your dad had an older sister."

"Diana! Of course!" Cassie had said. "I should have remembered. That explains the initials on the locket."

"She died," whispered Becky.

Cassie added, "But Dad never talks about her . . . "

"He — he can't. He adored her, and I don't think he ever really got over her death." She'd paused to phrase her words carefully. "It wasn't only the clothes. It seems that lately Becky looks and sounds more and more like his sister."

Becky had taken that badly. "Is that so awful?"

Cassie had never before seen her mother at a loss for words. "I — I can't say. Dad wants to tell you about her himself — when he's ready. Soon."

That was all they had been able to pry from her mother, and by the time Cassie had fallen asleep, she had still not heard her father emerge from his study.

Cassie was starting up the first steps leading up the cliff when Rumble tore past below her, chasing a rabbit into the undergrowth. Why does he even bother? Cassie thought idly. He hasn't a prayer of catching one. She watched him bound toward the underbrush at the rear of the boathouse. Suddenly he stopped dead, as if he'd hit a wall. He yelped.

Cassie hurried toward him, worried he had hurt himself, or cornered a fox. How would she break up a fight if she had to? she wondered. She ran closer. As she did, a rush of chill air hit her.

She looked around nervously. Alone here in the gloom of the desolate beach, inexplicably cold, listening to Rumble whine, she was suddenly afraid. But Rumble needed her. Cassie shook herself as if that could throw off the fear. But before she could move again Rumble bolted. He raced along the side of the boathouse and around the corner. Cassie followed as quickly as her sore ankle would allow. Just past the corner of the boathouse she could see Rumble running back and forth along the dock in a confused way. Each time he darted out, he was a little closer to the end of the dock. She'd better catch him before he jumped off into the lake. Her mother wouldn't appreciate her bringing home a sopping wet dog.

"It's all right, Rumble. Good boy. You're safe now. Come here, boy," she called from the beach, hoping not to have to step onto the shaky old dock.

Rumble had reached the dock's end, and was now pacing from one far corner to the other. She'd have to get him. She stepped onto the wooden planking. "Easy, Rumble, it's just me. C'mere now," she said, walking toward him. She leaned over to grab his collar, but as she touched him he jerked back. She lost her balance, tried to recover by shifting her feet, and felt her weak ankle buckle beneath her.

As she fell, her head cracked against the side of the dock. She rolled unconscious into the dark water.

CHAPTER 8

Cassie woke up looking into the blue eyes of Dorian Gzowski, and wondered if she was dead. Then she realized she was lying stretched out on the sand, wrapped in a warm sweater, "What happened?" she mumbled.

"You slipped on the dock and fell into the lake. I pulled you out. How's your head?"

Cassie shivered. Her clothes were wet. Water dripped from her hair onto her face, and she felt the grit of sand in her mouth. "I fell in the water? You saved my life?" She knew she sounded stupid, but her brain felt full of seaweed.

"Anyone would have done it."

Cassie nodded, then winced. Her head hurt as if a hammer were pounding it from the inside. She sat up slowly and rubbed her temples. Memory came flooding back. "Rumble . . . my dog — is he okay?"

"He's right behind you. He's fine now, but the

poor guy was really howling before. What happened to him?"

As soon as he heard his name Rumble leaned closer and whined happily. Cassie hugged him. "He probably got closer to a fox than he should have," she told Dorian. "He loves chasing them."

"Pretty dangerous sport."

Cassie nodded. But she didn't really think it had been a fox. Where had that rush of cold come from, that creepy feeling? She saw Dorian watching her with concern. "How did you get down here in time?" she asked.

"I was here already. Behind you. Sometimes I like walking the beach alone. I was just about to call you when your dog went nuts."

"Thanks. I'm lucky you were here."

He grinned at her. "Glad I could help." He pulled a strand of seaweed off her shoulder.

She looked down at her dripping clothes and muddy arms, and felt her head still throbbing. The girls in movies never look this awful when they're rescued, she thought. "I can get up now," she said.

"Can you walk? I should get you home."

Dorian reached out to help her up. She hesitated, too nervous to hold his hands.

"Take it slowly." Dorian slipped his arm around her waist and helped her to her feet.

Cassie tried to walk, but would have stumbled without Dorian's steady arm. Slowly they moved toward the wooden steps and began the long climb up the cliff. They had to stop twice to rest. Cassie was glad Dorian was behind her, his arm supportive. It occurred to her that in a romance novel, this would be a thrilling moment. She'd never be this close to him again. But everything felt too painful and unreal for her to savour it.

By the time they reached the house it was dark. Within minutes, her mother had Cassie wrapped in a blanket on the couch, sipping hot tea, while Dorian explained what had happened.

"Mother, please, I'm okay now," Cassie protested as her mother looked into her eyes and checked her head with experienced fingers.

"I'll keep a close watch on you tonight anyway," her mother said. "Tell me if you feel drowsy or nauseated. I want to be sure you don't have a concussion." She turned to Dorian and thanked him for his help.

Shortly after, Dorian said goodbye. As her mother walked him to the door, Cassie rested her aching head on the back of the couch and watched him leave. End of my romantic encounter, she thought wistfully.

Thursday it was Becky who hurried to the school bus and Cassie who was stuck home in bed. She'd insisted that she was all right, but when her mother cancelled her driving lesson and refused to let her go to school, she decided to enjoy the time and read *Wuthering Heights*, number nine on the "want to do" list she'd made before her birthday. But she couldn't concentrate. She kept drifting in and out of sleep, a sleep filled with hazy, unsettling dreams, like a series of music videos in fast-forward. She gathered impressions of music and dancing — a jumble of modern styles, old Elvis stuff, and even women in long gowns and men in formal suits floating around to the strains of Mozart and Strauss.

In some dreams, the dancers welcomed her. In others they turned away. Sometimes she danced with them, so full of joy she wanted to fly. Often she couldn't. No matter how hard she tried, or how desperately she pleaded, she couldn't reach the laughing dancers. Each time she woke up, she felt drained, exhausted, and bitterly cold.

Late in the afternoon, a loud slam of the kitchen door told her Becky was home from school. Moments later Becky thumped up the stairs and squealed into Cassie's room.

"Guess who came home with me! Dorian! He's worried about — "

"What? Augh. I look awful! Stall him." Cassie hurried to the bathroom, splashed water on her face and brushed her teeth and hair. Hanging on the door hook was her mother's blue silk robe. She glanced quickly at her own faded T-shirt night-gown, then grabbed the blue robe, pulling it on as she rushed back to her room into bed. Now her head ached.

She heard Becky and Dorian in the upstairs hall, and wished she looked frail and lovely, like a romantic heroine. But at least she was dressed elegantly, she thought, turning down the covers so that more of the blue silk would show.

"How are you today?" Dorian stood at the door. "You look better."

"I feel okay. I could have gone to school. It's just my parents . . . You know. Come in. Sit down." She pointed to the big chair beside her bed.

Dorian walked in and sat down. "You're lucky you weren't there today. Mr. Uchida called an assembly and gave a big lecture on smoking in the bathrooms."

Cassie groaned and rolled her eyes.

"Trouble is, the kids who need to hear it weren't there . . . "

Cassie finished his sentence with him. " . . . they were in the bathrooms, smoking."

Both of them laughed, then Cassie asked, "How was the soccer game today?"

"We won, three to two. Speaking of which . . . " He reached for his binder and pulled out an envelope, handing it to Cassie. "Your soccer shots. They're impressive."

Cassie felt disappointed. So *that* was why he was here. She opened the envelope and flipped through the photos. They weren't all great, but she was pleased with a few. She glanced at Dorian. He was looking at her photo of Seneca on the wall.

"That's a good picture, too. Is he yours?"

"No. I don't own him, but I ride him once or twice a week," she answered.

"You can really ride."

"Moi?"

"I watched you charging across the fields last Sunday."

"I didn't see you." If she had, she thought, she probably would've fallen off.

"You looked good," Dorian smiled at her warmly. Something in Cassie's chest fluttered and she wondered how it would feel to kiss that wonderful smile.

She told him about Seneca, then as he talked about a holiday he'd spent at a ranch once, she thought how easy he was to talk with. This is going so smoothly, she realized in amazement. Dorian had a way of gazing at her while he spoke that made her feel special.

He described his first horse ride, with such a hilarious description of his mistakes that she couldn't stop laughing. As she laughed, she saw him watching her again. She looked down self-consciously, and stared in horror. What was that on her sleeve? A seam? Oh, no! A seam with dark threads sprouting around it. She was wearing the glamorous silk robe inside out.

She wanted to slide under her covers. How could she have been so stupid? Here she thought she looked sophisticated, that the visit was going so well, and all the while her robe was on inside out, threads and lining and all. No wonder Dorian had stared at her — he couldn't believe she was such an idiot. Had he been laughing at her all along?

" . . . and that persuaded me to stick with cars," Dorian finished his story. It was her turn to speak, but she couldn't think of a word to say. She masked her confusion with a cool expression, but she wondered if her face was burning every shade of red.

As the silence lengthened, Cassie figured Dorian would surely get up and leave. But he sat, saying nothing, until she finally looked at him. She was surprised to see how uncertain he appeared. He was obviously stuck for words too. Then to her amazement, he blushed.

She couldn't believe it! He must have assumed he'd said something wrong — and he was blushing! She'd never liked him more than at this moment. She giggled.

He grinned, picked up her woollen slipper and tossed it at her. She threw it back and dodged sideways, just as he leaned over to retrieve it. Their faces came so close, she could feel his warm breath . . .

She moved back, and began straightening her pillows. Dorian carefully placed her slipper beside the other one on the floor.

There was an awkward silence. They both glanced at the pile of soccer photos on Cassie's bed, then spoke at the same time.

"Where did you — ?"

"How did you — ?"

They laughed. "You go first," suggested Cassie.

"Where did you learn to shoot like that? Not just anyone gets pictures as good as those," Dorian said.

"My dad taught me, photographing Rumble as a pup. It's been special ever since. How did you get the soccer shots?"

"Maya gave them to Mrs. McNicoll, the yearbook advisor. She's thrilled. Says you'll add class to the yearbook. I promised to beg you to join us. She wants to ask you herself tomorrow, but I told her I was coming here anyway."

She shifted in bed to hide her happy smile. So it wasn't just the photos that had brought him. "But your illustrations already look great in the book," she said.

"They're just cartoons. Photographs are different."

"Just cartoons? I recognize everyone you draw. And the humour's right on."

"You like my stuff?"

"Like it? I envy you. How long have you been drawing?"

"Forever. My mum has pictures I drew since I could hold a crayon." He laughed shyly, while Cassie wondered if her mother liked anything she did, enough to save.

"I'd like to see more some time," Cassie said, then blushed. What was it about Dorian that made all her words come out so corny?

He looked at her, and apparently decided she was sincere. He twirled an invisible moustache and tried to sound French. "One fine evening, mademoiselle, you must come up to my place to see my etchings."

Cassie laughed. He really was too nice to go all silly over. And far too good to use to show off to other girls like a charm on an expensive bracelet.

"I've got to go. I'm glad you're all right, Cassie. See you tomorrow if you're back at school then."

She walked him downstairs to the door, then danced back to the kitchen. Only when she got back to her room did she remember the inside-out bathrobe.

Just after dinner Becky announced another visitor. She grinned like a leprechaun as Cassie demanded how many people knew about her accident, and just how awful Becky had made it sound. She went to the living room where Ben sat. A crumpled bunch of yellow mums lay on the coffee table beside him. Cassie thought he looked half proud he'd brought them, and half embarrassed.

"I see you're going to live." He grinned.

"You know my blockhead . . . Um — the flowers are beautiful."

"Yeah, my mum picked them." He played with his school ring awhile. "Are you back at school tomorrow?"

"Yeah. I should be . . . " It was an uncomfortable

visit. Cassie couldn't figure out why that was happening to them lately. They'd been friends for so long. They used to talk about everything, and now she couldn't tell him how much those flowers meant to her. She knew neither of them could handle that. When Ben left after only ten minutes, she was almost relieved.

Next day, Maya dragged Cassie to the yearbook "office," one of the glassed-in study rooms off the library. Huge travel posters of Africa covered the windows for privacy. Maya introduced her to Mrs. McNicoll.

"Cassie!" The yearbook advisor grinned. "Your photos are terrific — crisp, clever and centred. I'm absolutely delighted with them."

"I — Thank you." Cassie blushed.

Maya and Mrs. McNicoll took turns complimenting her photographs as if the entire yearbook would fail without them.

"A professional takes all our individual and team pictures," Mrs. McNicoll explained. "We need you for the candid shots — special events, ordinary scenes from a new angle — that kind of thing. We meet Tuesdays at lunch, every Friday afternoon just like now, and whenever something special comes up. It's a lot of fun. Will you join us?"

"If you don't, the yearbook is doomed to carry my sky and headless people shots," Maya warned.

They both looked at Cassie like beagles waiting for a bone.

She didn't know what to think. She loved taking pictures, but they didn't always turn out. What if the rest of the kids didn't like the photos? They'd be in the yearbook forever.

She wanted to do this . . . and yet she didn't.

She looked at her friend. Maya had urged her to join them for a long time. Dorian had mentioned it too. She thought of Dorian and imagined working side by side with him every Tuesday and Friday afternoon.

Loud laughter from a group of students in the library interrupted her thoughts — Mark Murdoch's voice. She listened to his friends laughing. She'd have to attend all the special events — crowded dances, games, club meetings, pep rallies. She'd have to butt in everywhere to get good shots, and approach people for their names and everything.

Mark spotted her through the doorway and mimed a rude dance. His friends laughed again, but Cassie went cold. She knew she couldn't do it.

"I'm sorry," she stammered, "I often baby-sit Friday nights when most of the stuff would be happening . . . "

She hated the look of disappointment in Maya's face, and was glad when Maya turned away to work at a cluttered table.

Mrs. McNicoll flipped through the rest of her

mail. She tossed two envelopes into the blue recycling box, slit open a large brown one, and smiled at Cassie. "That's too bad, Cassie. The offer's open if you change your mind. In the meantime, you'll let us use the soccer shots, won't you? They really are excellent."

Relieved, Cassie nodded yes.

Mrs. McNicoll smiled again. "I understand you're busy, but would you mind, just as a last-minute favour, taking a couple of shots of the student council elections Monday afternoon? I already have the candidates' names. Just this once."

Cautiously, Cassie agreed. Mrs. McNicoll pulled two rolls of film from a shelf and handed them to her. As Cassie turned to leave she almost bumped into Ben, staggering in under a load of boxes.

"Ah, good," said Ben. "You've finally joined us."

"No, I didn't. But since when have *you* worked here, you little overachiever?" She knew she sounded sarcastic because she was angry at herself. Why couldn't she just join the yearbook staff without worrying so much about it? This seemed like a friendly place.

"I started this year. Have to. College scholarships go to all-around students. Looks good on my resumé too. I don't do much — just sell advertising space."

"Don't believe that, Cassie. He's the best salesman we ever had," said Mrs. McNicoll.

"Your smooth talking gets you everywhere, Mrs.

Mick. Where do you want these boxes?"

"On that counter, thanks, Ben," said Mrs. McNicoll. Then to Cassie she said offhandedly. "If you happen to have any film left over, could you just use it up at the next soccer game, and maybe in the cafeteria? I hate to waste it."

"If there's any left," Cassie answered slowly. She knew very well there'd be lots. Ben was right about Mrs. McNicoll, she realized as she left the office. I have this feeling she's just smooth-talked me onto the yearbook staff. Funny, but I'm sort of glad.

At four o'clock, Cassie was surprised to see Dorian waiting at her locker. He looked tall, blond and wonderful — and very nervous.

"Can I talk to you alone?" he asked. "I'll walk you to the bus."

Cassie forced herself to sound casual. "Have I taken the wrong pictures already?"

"This isn't funny."

Cassie dreaded what was coming.

CHAPTER 9

As they walked to the bus, Dorian pushed his hands in and out of his pockets and cleared his throat so often Cassie wanted to scream at him to start talking.

Finally he did. "I heard a dumb rumour about you last Monday and put it off as a bad joke. But yesterday some guys in the gym started again. They said they saw you in the back room at Beachball's Pizza — acting really wild."

Cassie felt sick. Was this ever going to stop?

"They said you were out in the middle of the dance floor, showing off every move."

That's so ridiculous, Cassie thought. How could anyone believe she'd do that? She wished Dorian would stop saying "you."

As if he'd read her mind, he added, "I know it wasn't you, Cassie. They were talking about Wednesday night, and Wednesday night you were on the beach with me, then at home."

They had reached the bus. As they climbed the steps Cassie spotted Shauna glaring at them. "Oh Dorian, you're here." Shauna's voice was honey but her look at Cassie was acid. "I've saved a seat for you."

Dorian waved at her, then leaned close to tell Cassie softly, "Something isn't right. That wasn't you. But hey, don't worry. They'll figure it out soon." Then he joined Shauna in the seat she guarded in that special back section.

I'm being dumb, thought Cassie, as she looked for somewhere to sit. It wasn't as if they'd put up a sign excluding everyone but the in-crowd, but no one else sat there anyway. She'd always assumed she could if she wanted to — but now? Cassie wondered what they'd do if she and her new reputation plopped down right next to them.

Instead, she sat beside Ben, fuming. She didn't deserve this. If she could just get her hands on that — that lookalike everyone assumed was her!

"I'm glad you're taking pictures for the yearbook, Cass," Ben said. "You'll like it."

"Why didn't you tell me you were working there too?" Cassie asked. They used to tell each other things like that.

Ben shrugged his shoulders. "Guess I figured it didn't matter."

"Since when don't I care what you do?"

"You're kinda preoccupied lately."

"Sorry. Am I? Have I been awful?"

74

"You awful? Never." Cassie couldn't tell if he was joking or not, but she felt better.

He began to talk about the yearbook, but her thoughts soon drifted back to Dorian's story. Who was this dancing sideshow? Why were people so ready to believe it was her? Didn't they remember she had never acted that tacky in her life? She wished she could just shrug it off, but it made her feel creepy.

Ben had stopped talking. She looked up. Uh oh — from his eager expression she assumed he was waiting for an answer. "Uh — sure," she guessed.

"Great. Think how fantastic a video yearbook would be. Imagine the possibilities — moving, talking memories instead of those little flat photos."

He began planning aloud, but Cassie could only think about the girl who flaunted it around the dance floors. Why had no one ever noticed her before? Had she just moved here? It wasn't that big a town, so sooner or later they were bound to run into each other.

Ben had paused again. "Um, me too," she said quickly.

He looked at her oddly, then reached for his backpack. "Guess I'll start this math now. I have to work tonight."

Oh no, she'd done it again. What had Ben asked? Perhaps he too had heard the latest rumour, and all this talk about the yearbook was just to cover up. Great, now she was getting suspicious about her own friend. She was relieved when the bus stopped at Greystones.

It was after nine o'clock. Becky was out at a movie with Erin, and her mother was on emergency room duty. Cassie had just finished a letter to Dan. It was too bad he had picked a college on the other side of the country. She needed him here to talk to — he always made sense of everything. She had considered writing him about the weird things happening to her, but what could he do from so far away?

Maya must be home from work now, she thought — the drugstore closed at nine. She dialled Maya's number.

As soon as she heard her friend's voice she asked, "Maya, what's wrong?"

"My grandmother — she's really sick."

"The nice one who visits you every summer? Will she be all right?"

"I think so, but we don't really know. It's so hard to find out anything when you have to go through overseas operators, different time zones and emotional relatives."

"I never thought of that. I guess I was lucky to have my grandparents so close."

"Mum's worried and uptight, and Dad's saying all the wrong things. I can't stand being home right now."

Cassie didn't have the heart to burden Maya

further with her problems, but before she could think of another reason for calling, Maya asked how she was doing. She tried to toss off a glib answer. "Oh, I'm fine, except that my dancing double's appeared again."

"You're kidding! Where?"

"Beachball's, so the rumour says. I can't believe it, Maya. If I could just catch sight of her myself . . . "

"Come on over tomorrow night. We'll hang around town a bit — see if we can spot her."

"Great idea. Why didn't I think of that?"

As they planned where they would go, Cassie's father came to her door. He smiled at Cassie, but he looked tired, his face pale against his dark hair.

"It's been a tough week at work. Do you have time to join me for a cup of tea?"

"Let me finish making plans with Maya, Dad. Five minutes."

Awhile later Cassie found her dad making tea in the kitchen. They carried their mugs and cookies down the hall, Rumble trotting behind them, heading for the music room. Dan had named it that long ago because of the ancient baby grand piano it contained. The room looked almost Victorian, with several palm and fern plants, lots of lace, and a couple of overstuffed chintz couches. Behind the piano, two floor-length windows faced out to the dark front lawn.

Her dad put a CD in the machine while Cassie curled up on her favourite couch. She recognized the music as Mozart. She'd heard it enough. They listened to the music and talked comfortably. She wanted to ask him about Diana, but was afraid to spoil the peaceful mood. His reaction Tuesday night had really frightened her. Instead she answered his questions about school work, and told him her news. "I've been asked to join the yearbook committee, Dad."

"Taking photographs?"

"How'd you know?"

"Easy — you're good at it. Congratulations, Cassie. I'm proud of you."

She was surprised to realize she felt proud too.

"What kind of camera do they use?" her dad asked. Rumble trotted in to join them and curled up by Cassie's feet. She stroked his head absently while she and her father chatted about the photography for awhile. Gradually their conversation drifted away as the music played. A gentle rain began to keep time with it on the window panes.

They barely heard the phone ringing in the distance. With a frown her dad got up to answer it. When he had not returned several minutes later, she knew it was another business call. He never escapes it for long, she thought, sinking back against the cushions.

She slipped back into her relaxed state. In small doses this music was decent. Her eyes closed. A warm full feeling began to flow through her. The rain pattered on the window and the music played on easily. She drifted almost into sleep.

A sudden chill roused her. She curled herself deeper into the cushions, half aware of a faint scent of roses. The cold deepened, and the contented fullness Cassie had been feeling just moments before intensified, overwhelming her. She was almost choking with it.

She opened her eyes in panic. She tried to get up, but her body was limp. She couldn't move! A fierce sense of danger engulfed her. She felt as if she were caught in a mud slide, cold black slime streaming over her, surrounding her, sucking her in and oozing into her eyes, her nose, her mouth.

But there was nothing to see in the dim room, nothing except Rumble, standing tense, every hair bristling. He growled deep in his throat. Cassie felt as if some invisible thing was attacking her, invading her body and her will.

CHAPTER 10

She wanted to scream, to run, but she lay totally helpless. The weaker she became, the stronger the force pushed, until she thought she had no room left to breathe.

What was happening? She couldn't see anything unusual, not even a shadow. The only sound was her own short gasps of breath. But there was a smell — too sweet, too heavy — of summer roses.

She willed herself to resist the force. But it was inside her, and she didn't know how to push it back. Slowly, steadily, the force was taking over each limb, every muscle. Was this how it felt to become paralyzed?

Twin bright beams of light pierced the room. Headlights! Becky had come home. The thing invading Cassie paused. A car door slammed. Shouts of goodbye filled the night. As the beams of bright light still shone, the force invading Cassie began to ebb.

The sound of the doorbell chimes echoed through the house. "Dad!" Cassie heard her sister calling, "Hey, Cassie! Let me in. It's raining out here!"

As the shrill ringing continued, the force stopped. Cassie's arms and legs tingled as if they had been asleep. It was gone. Just like that. And so was the smell of roses. Cassie couldn't believe this had ended. Or that it had happened at all.

Unsteadily she went to the door to let her sister in.

"It's about time. It's wet out here."

"Go change into dry clothes. I'll make some hot chocolate," Cassie croaked. She needed something hot more than Becky did.

"You're fussing about *my* health, and you sound like that?" Becky said, and ran upstairs.

In the kitchen, Cassie turned on every light, and found a loud rock station on the radio. She cupped her hands around her warm mug as if it were a life preserver. She was relieved when Becky came in wearing pyjamas, bursting with cheery news.

Becky leaned on the kitchen counter, spread peanut butter on crackers and described her evening in happy non-stop detail. Their dad joined them, apologizing to Cassie for the long phone call.

Cassie didn't really listen to all they said, but she wanted the company and as much light as possible, to thaw out the ice-cold spot inside her.

How normal we all look and sound, she thought. But something terrible is going on. She was still shaking so much inside she was surprised Becky and her father didn't notice. She wanted to talk about her horrifying experience, but what would she say? It sounded unbelievable. She herself wasn't even sure what had just happened.

Finally she could sit still no longer. She excused herself, slipped upstairs to her room and picked up the phone. Maya's line was busy each time she dialled. Hopefully, they were getting good news about her grandmother. She tried Ben's number. When the answering machine clicked on, she hung up and went to bed. Leaving her lights and music on, she lay awake for a long time, until she warmed up enough to sleep.

Even then Cassie slept badly. This time there was only one strange dream. The old-fashioned men and women still floated around to the music of Mozart and Strauss. Tonight they were dancing in the Greystones ballroom as it must have appeared long ago. At first the dancers beckoned and smiled at her. Soon they regarded her with disapproval. They waltzed away from her, stepping and swirling in graceful closed circles. She tried to reach them, but her legs were too heavy to move. She called out to them, but the music and laughter drowned out her cries.

Then she was outside the ballroom, hovering desperately at the French doors. She knocked on the glass, then pounded and shouted, but not one of the dancers even looked her way . . .

When muffled sounds above her woke Cassie up on Saturday morning, it took her a moment to separate them from her dream. She lay in bed, listening. Was it footsteps? Her room was under the second attic. Diana's attic.

She shifted nervously. The footsteps echoed on the attic stairs, down the hall and toward her room. Cassie shot up in bed and clutched her covers to her chest, rigid.

Then the footsteps passed by, and she felt silly. It was only her mother and Roger, the interior decorator, on their way downstairs, talking about their latest project. Cassie threw aside her covers and almost ran for the shower, eager to wash away the events of last night and her exhausting dream.

An hour later she finished breakfast in the kitchen and read the paper, half-listening to Roger and her mother.

"Even the frames are still in excellent condition. Quality does endure, Ellen. I'd like to hang them on the long wall above the front landing. They'd be perfect there."

"An ancestral gallery? Sounds awfully Gothic, Roger."

He spread his arms wide. "They'll add such an aura of history, distinction — "

"Pomposity."

Cassie looked up to catch the offended look on Roger's face. Cassie's mother laughed it away. "Just kidding, Roger. Let's try it. We can always send them back up to the attic again." She turned to Cassie. "Your driving lesson is at two o'clock. Are you going straight to Maya's after that? You're staying over, right? The instructor can drop you off in town."

Cassie stared at her mother. Her brown streaked hair was pulled back in a neat ponytail, her skin fresh without make-up, and her clothes casual and perfect. She looked crisp and alert, not at all like someone who had spent most of the night working at the hospital.

But then action and drama always did more for her mother than eight hours sleep, thought Cassie as she rubbed her own tired eyes. Sometimes she found her mother's restless energy annoying — they all did, making jokes about Whirlwind Ellie.

"Cassie . . . Hello, Cassie," her mother was saying impatiently.

"Uh — what? Oh. Yes, okay. I'll pack my riding clothes, but will you bring my boots and helmet to the barn with Becky tomorrow?"

"Just be there on time please." Barely pausing for breath, she turned back to Roger. "I have some ideas for the old ballroom. Did you bring the wall-paper samples I suggested?"

Cassie glanced at the portraits lined up in a row against the kitchen cupboards. Stern gentlemen in tight collars and stiff ladies in corseted gowns stared glassily at no one. But the last one startled her. A girl about her age, with red-gold hair streaming out of control, looked directly at Cassie with bright eyes and a mocking smile.

"Wow," she said aloud. "Look at that one." The artist had been good. The girl looked so alive Cassie almost expected her to burst out of the frame. Could this be Diana — the sister her father wouldn't talk about? She looked restless, electric, eager for trouble. But no. The clothes dated this portrait back to the last century. Diana had lived in the nineteen-forties and -fifties.

"Yes, that one is different, isn't it?" Cassie's mother walked over to the portrait and studied it. "She looks like you, Cassie. But a little more . . . " Her mother's voice trailed off but Cassie had not missed the meaning. She'd been compared to the vivacious girl in the portrait . . . and lost the contest.

That's standard. No matter what she's talking about, she manages to criticize me, thought Cassie. I don't care. I'm happy as I am. She shrugged her shoulders in the way she knew her mother hated.

Becky bounced in from outside, red-cheeked and smiling. "I need a warmer jacket — it feels like winter out there already."

Her mother started to fuss over her, but Becky spotted the picture and interrupted. "Hey, freaky.

That one looks just like Cassie." She stopped and thought. "Only . . . wilder."

Et tu, Becky, thought Cassie ruefully. Without a word she headed upstairs to pack for Maya's.

As soon as Cassie came in the front door Sunday afternoon, she agreed with her mother's comment. The portraits, now hanging in the hall at the top of the curved staircase, did look pompous. She shrugged. Oh well, so did a few other things around here, like the stained-glass window darkening the dining room, and the stone lions guarding the driveway. She wished they could guard her.

She went upstairs. Oops. A picture had fallen. She squatted to pick it up, and inspected it for damage. The saucy familiar face surprised her again. It was the girl with the wild red-gold hair. Cassie hung it back up and straightened it carefully, trying to ignore the taunting eyes.

Becky had followed her up. "So how was Maya's?"

"Good. We went to Beachball's, then watched a video." They had walked around town until late, but found no one who looked like Cassie. At least she'd been able to share the burden of the frightening incident in the music room. She'd stumbled her way through the telling of it. It sounded too weird even to her, but Maya had listened attentively.

"Amazing," Maya had said when Cassie was done.

"Do you think I — imagined it?" Cassie had to ask.

"You're not exactly the feverish imagination type," Maya answered.

"Then what am I? Going crazy?"

Maya laughed. "Hardly. You're the sanest person I know. But . . . "

"But what?"

"Well, it's really weird . . . Give me time to think about this some more. I'll tell you then." Quickly she had changed the subject. "I saw Dorian watching you during the yearbook meeting on Friday," she teased. "I bet he likes you."

"Only in your fertile imagination and my dreams, Maya. Why would the most popular guy in school be interested in me?"

"Maybe he's glad to find a girl who doesn't drool all over him — or want him as a trophy."

"Oh, Maya. If only it were true. He is *so* nice," Cassie had said wistfully.

Now Becky looked with Cassie at the portrait on the wall. "That's funny. I hung that picture back up this morning too," she said. "It needs a stronger hook."

They both stepped back to study the troublesome painting. "She's so beautiful," sighed Cassie.

Becky looked at her oddly. "She looks like you, Cassie. She's just . . . bolder."

Cassie hadn't forgotten how hurt she'd felt yesterday. "Thanks, Becky," she said softly.

"She looks like she'd have been some fun," Becky went on.

"Maybe too much fun. I wonder what happened to her." Cassie shivered. Had Becky noticed the slight scent of roses in the air?

For the next two weeks, school life was back to normal for Cassie. Except for one wonderful thing. Every day, somewhere, she would run into Dorian. He'd be in line behind her in the cafeteria, next to her in the hall, or sitting beside her during the yearbook meetings. Each time, Cassie was amazed how easily they could talk. Other guys had always made her too nervous — except good old Ben of course — but there seemed to be so much to talk about with Dorian. They discovered they liked most of the same music and books, disliked the same classes, and argued cheerfully about the state of the world.

After lunch one day, they carried their Cokes down to the trees past the sports fields. They walked under a canopy of colour-crazy maples, and watched the sun-dappled patterns on the crimson and gold leaves on the ground. Cassie thought October had never looked so bright and glorious.

They talked about the new wing under construction at the hospital. "Mother's in her glory," laughed Cassie. "The renovations at Greystones are almost finished, so now she's happily advising the architect about efficient hospital layouts."

Dorian laughed too. "My dad wouldn't notice unless a brick fell on his operating table."

Shauna and her friends passed by, glowering at them. Cassie smiled secretly and was surprised at herself. When she glanced across the field and saw Ben jogging around the track, she felt terrible, and was surprised by that too.

She remembered Ben's "hotshot surgeon" theory, and decided to test it. "What about you, Dorian? Will you be a doctor too?"

He said nothing for awhile, and finally answered carefully. "It's in the blood I guess. I'll be the fourth generation of doctors in my family. But not here."

He stopped, and she smiled encouragingly. Almost shyly, he continued, "I want to be more than some preppie doing the right things in the right places with the right people."

He stopped again, checking her reaction. In a moment he continued. "Sometimes I think I have it so easy, I don't even know how easy I've got it. I want to help those who don't."

"Like Africa or Asia?"

"Maybe. But I was thinking about here, in the inner cities. Then I can be happy driving home in my sports car at the end of the day. What about you?"

"Wish I knew. I love photography, but medicine fascinates me more. I'll probably end up spying on viruses through a microscope. 'Hiding out with the other laboratory mice,' my mother calls it, but I'd like to discover the cure for a major disease or something."

Awhile later, as they walked back to the school, he invited her to go to a movie with him on Saturday night.

Cassie was so surprised she almost asked him to repeat himself. She wanted to jump up, cheer, dance around. Instead she pulled herself together and casually agreed. Then she almost forgot to say goodbye as he headed for the gym and she floated to her locker. She kept thinking — a whole evening with Dorian. Beside Dorian. Dorian and her. How would she survive until Saturday night?

Had she been thinking less about Dorian, her life at home would have bothered her more. There had been no more invisible visitors, so that fear was gone, but she kept falling asleep early and at odd times of the day. She had skipped riding last Sunday, turned down a baby-sitting job, even forgot to show up for a yearbook meeting. Whenever her father suggested a driving lesson, she yawned and used having too much homework as an excuse. Even doing her homework seemed a huge effort, and her frequent headaches made it hard to concentrate. Her mother made pointed remarks about her laziness, but Cassie felt too weary to argue with her.

That was why she didn't feel like sharing news of her date with her mother, even though it was her first one. Daughters were supposed to share stuff like this with their mothers. Instead, she hugged her happiness to herself, and changed her mind about what to wear at least ten times.

So she knew her mother was surprised, Saturday night, to answer the door to Dorian Gzowski. She was pleasant, but Cassie saw the hurt in her eyes.

She tried not to think about it as they walked to Dorian's car. Then she forgot it. The night she had wished for was happening. She was going out with Dorian.

The evening was clear and cool. A lazy yellow moon smiled down at her from an incredibly beautiful star-sprinkled sky. Nothing could spoil this date.

Dorian turned his car in the driveway. He waved back at her mother standing in the lighted doorway.

Cassie waved too. When her mother closed the door, she began to turn toward Dorian, but a slight movement caught her eye. She looked above the doorway to an upstairs window. It was not as dark as the others — a pale light seemed to shimmer from it. It must be the moon reflecting in the glass, she thought. Then she froze. Framed in the window was a shadowy image, a girl who seemed surrounded by clouds of streaming hair.

As the car picked up speed, the figure almost seemed to stare directly down at Cassie. Did Cassie see, or did she imagine, the jealousy and hatred flashing from those eyes?

It was the girl who looked like her. The girl in the ancient picture.

CHAPTER 11

Cassie clutched the car door armrest hard to keep from screaming. In an instant, the hazy figure disappeared. The window was left black and ominous.

Dorian began to talk about the movie. Had she imagined the girl? Had it been merely a trick of moonlight and the shadows of quivering tree branches? The queasy, panicky ache in her stomach said no. She turned to Dorian to ask him to take her back home, then hesitated. What would she say? Hey Dorian, I think I saw some dead girl from an old painting standing at the window. Or, gee Dorian, I just remembered I feel too sick to go out. She'd look like an idiot.

He smiled at her. That wonderful smile. Those blue eyes. It's not fair, she thought. This was supposed to be my dream evening.

No! She decided. I'm not ruining this date because of some shadows in a dark window. I'll check it later when I get home and find out it was the reflection of the moon or a hall light or something. Maybe Mom got tired of the portrait falling down all the time, and stuck it upstairs, right by that window. I have a date with Dorian and I'm going to enjoy it.

But she soon began to feel she should have stayed home. Whenever Dorian spoke to her, she had to ask him to repeat it. Everyone around her laughed at the movie, while Cassie couldn't even follow the plot. The popcorn Dorian brought her stuck dry in her mouth, so she put the still full bag down on the floor beside her. At the restaurant afterwards, she couldn't eat, and was glad when a bunch of others joined them so she didn't have to think of anything to say. It was as if something had sucked all the joy out of the evening, leaving her dazed and empty.

Almost empty, for she kept thinking about the figure in the window. She had hardly seen it, and only for an instant. Yet, as the evening plodded on, it became clearer and clearer, imprinting itself like a photograph in her mind.

Cassie couldn't stand the look in Dorian's eyes when they got in the car to drive home. Their date had been a disaster. And it was her fault. As Dorian walked her to the door, she thought she'd burst with frustration. She glared at the upstairs window. It was dark and empty.

"Good night, Cassie." Dorian faced her uncertainly. How could she explain to him what had happened, when she didn't know herself?

"Good night, Dorian," she stammered. "I had a good time." It sounded lame, even to her, and Dorian responded equally lamely. He walked to his car without looking back. Cassie stood watching until his headlights died in the black distance, then walked slowly inside.

"Cassie? How was your evening?"

Her mother stood in the hallway. The forced lightness in her tone and the uncertainty in her eyes finished Cassie. Unable to hold back the tears any longer, she ran up to her room.

For a long while she sobbed into her pillows. She neither heard her mother's tentative knock, nor felt the sudden chill in her room. Finally exhausted, she slept.

Daylight streaming into her room the next morning almost made last night seem impossible. But no amount of sunshine could make Cassie forget the miserable hunch of Dorian's shoulders as he walked back to his car.

Her door crashed open. A white shape flew across the room and bounced onto her bed. "How was the dream date? Where did you go? Did you hold hands? Did he kiss you?"

As usual, Becky never paused long enough for answers. When she finally stopped for breath, Cassie could truthfully say, "He's pretty wonderful," and smile mysteriously.

Becky began to dream aloud about her first date. Cassie listened for awhile, then interrupted, "When did you get home last night?"

"Ten-thirty. We had to wait for Jenna's dad."

"So you definitely weren't here when Dorian picked me up?"

"You saw me leave."

"None of your friends were here?"

"Why would my friends be here without me? Boy, are you weird lately."

Just checking every angle, thought Cassie. It hadn't been a guest of her parents or one of Roger's workmen either, but she'd double-check with Mother anyway.

Mother! Cassie thought of her waiting up last night, and the hurt in her eyes. They'd have to talk about it sooner or later. But not yet. Should she mention the girl in the window to her mother? She almost laughed at the thought. "Is Mother up?" she asked.

"At the hospital. Emergency appendectomy."

For now she was spared. Cassie skipped breakfast and phoned Maya. Briefly she explained last night's disastrous date. Then, deciding Maya wouldn't call her crazy, she described what she'd seen in the window. The line went silent. Cassie could almost see Maya straighten her glasses and think.

"And you're sure it looked like the girl from the painting?" asked Maya.

"I don't know anybody else who has that wild-looking hair."

There was another silence on the line, then Maya spoke again. "Cassie, don't think I've flipped out, but after what you told me before, I got reading and . . . I think you have a ghost."

"Get real. A ghost? That's the answer I get from a science major?"

"I've wondered about this ever since you told me what happened in the music room. Think about it, Cassie. The portrait came from your attic, so she's obviously an ancestor of yours, still roaming about her home. I always thought Greystones was the perfect setting for a haunting."

"Come on, Maya. I don't believe in ghosts."

"Neither do I, but I sure can't disbelieve either. An awful lot of people claim they've seen one."

"That's ridiculous. No one's ever been able to prove it."

"How many more hundreds of eyewitness accounts do we need? And there are photos . . ."

"Touched-up fakes."

"Even if most of them are, that still leaves some that can't be explained away. Serious, scientific research is going on about the paranormal these days."

"But there's still no definite proof." Cassie knew she was arguing too much. She had to. She didn't want this to be true. "Maya, there's no such thing as a ghost."

"Maybe. Maybe not. I've read that a ghost isn't

an actual thing, but an event, like a fire."

"Whatever." Why am I arguing? Maya's right, thought Cassie. Whatever this thing is, it's having some kind of effect on me, and I want it to stop. "Okay," she said at last. "I find it hard to believe, but let's say it's true. Then at least we have something to fight."

"We'd improve our chances if we knew what, or who, we were up against," said Maya thoughtfully.

"Then we need to find out whose ghost this is," Cassie said. "And why she's here."

"The first is easy — we have a portrait to go by. There has to be some information about it somewhere. Didn't your grandfather know all about your family tree? Did he tell you any stories about her?"

"I can't remember any."

"Why don't you ask your parents?"

"My dad's home now. I'll talk to him and call you right back."

Her father's study was a sleek square built into the east section of what was once the ballroom. Cassie stood at the entrance, remembering the dancing figures in her dreams. Had they meant anything? She knocked at the study door and entered.

Surrounded by his piles of charts and reports, absorbed by the computer screen, it took her father a moment to notice her.

"Dad. The girl in the hall picture — is she Diana?" She hoped to surprise an answer from him.

He looked up, startled. "No! Diana was lovelier . . . more gentle. She was a sweet girl before . . . Why do you ask?"

"I'm fascinated by it."

"Don't be." Her father seemed agitated. He rolled his chair back and forth. "I mean . . . it's such a nuisance. It keeps falling down. I've told Roger to get rid of it before the wall is ruined."

"You loved Diana a lot."

He smiled a little. "I adored her. She was a wonderful sister."

"What happened to her, Dad?" It was the first time Cassie had dared to ask.

Ashen faced, her father pushed back in his chair again. Instantly the computer screen went blank. Cassie glanced from it to the floor, where the chair wheels had caught the cord and pulled the plug from the wall socket.

"My work! I've lost three hours' work. I can't talk now, Cassie. This report is due tomorrow!"

"But Dad — "

"We'll talk another time Cassie, please." He scrambled around, replugging the cord and pressing buttons.

Cassie gave up and left the room. Her father's timing had been too neat. As she shut the study door, she heard him mutter, "Diana loathed that picture."

Just as she was about to call Maya back, it occurred to Cassie that Roger might know about the portrait. He was the one who had suggested the ancestors gallery. She located his card by the phone and dialled his number.

This time she was in luck. Roger did know a little about it. "The artist was August Bellingham Saint Claire — very talented, and quite a dandy. I think his career began around 1890. He painted wealthy young ladies across North America," Roger told her. Then he laughed. "Fathers and husbands were usually glad to see the back of Saint Claire. Seems he was a bit of a . . . Well, anyway, he must have caused one scandal too many, because he left for Paris quite suddenly. I know he was painting there by 1899."

"Do you know who the girl in our picture is?"

"No. I thought your parents might, but they didn't seem to. Maybe your grandparents would have known, but . . . "

Discouraged, Cassie was about to thank Roger and hang up when he said, "There is someplace you might find out."

"Where?"

"There's a book. There are several featuring Greystones, but this one has some bits about the Dennings. Now what is it called?" He paused. "History of . . . Early Families . . . *First Families of Port Morden!* I'm sure that's it. The library should have a copy."

Cassie thanked him and quickly phoned Maya.

Maya sounded as excited as Cassie felt. "Will

your dad drive you in? Tell him we'll treat you to McDonald's and bring you home later."

As they drove into town, Cassie glanced out over the lake. The waves had turned choppy. A mass of dark clouds and its shadow, black on the water, raced toward them faster than seemed possible. "It started out so sunny this morning. Now look at the sky."

Her dad nodded. "Don't stay too late. We'll have a storm by tonight."

Minutes later they pulled into the parking lot of the ivy-covered red brick library. Cassie said good-bye to her father and met Maya inside. She was already talking to the librarian.

"Yes. We have several books with photos and drawings of our area's lovely old homes, but *First Families of Port Morden* has the best history of the people." The librarian pointed toward a shelf near the back. "They're over there."

There were several copies. Cassie and Maya each grabbed one and leafed through the pages until they got to the Dennings. "Check between 1890 and 1899," said Cassie.

A small black-and-white family photo caught her eye and she began to tremble. She knew the girl standing to the left. The caption listed only a date — 1894 — and the names. Which name belonged to the girl on the left? Cassie counted the figures. Catherine. Her name was Catherine. Cassie and Maya looked at each other, without saying it. She and the girl in the portrait had the same name!

Quickly Cassie scanned the page for more information. It listed Edward Denning's accomplishments — businessman, mayor, elder of the Presbyterian Church, founder of various clubs and a park, and so on. All but the church work ended abruptly in 1895. "Family troubles" had been the only reason given. Then the book moved on to the eldest of Edward's sons. There was little about the rest of the family, and nothing about Catherine.

Cassie slapped the table in frustration, and the pages flipped to the end. The last picture in the book was on the back lawn at Greystones. She recognized again the younger version of her grandparents, and a girl and a younger boy, laughing in the sunlight. Cassie almost cried. They looked so happy then — her grandparents, her father, and Diana.

Maya had turned to the front of her book and was skimming the table of contents and the introduction. Suddenly she stopped. "Cassie, look at this."

Cassie read the paragraph Maya pointed to. The author was thanking all the people who had helped her research the book: Cassie's grandfather was included, of course. And then she saw the name Diana. Diana Denning had been an invaluable and enthusiastic assistant, digging through hundreds of old letters and public records.

The last paragraph was a tribute. The author was grieved to note that shortly before the book was published, Diana had been killed by a truck while crossing Main Street. The writer praised how lovely and intelligent, how full of life and promise Diana had been, what a great loss her death was to her parents, her beloved brother Tommy, to Port Morden and the world.

The two girls sat still for a long moment. Now Cassie knew why Tommy — Tom, her father — so often seemed sad.

The heavy oak doors of the library were harder to open than usual. The wind pushed hard against them. Outside it seemed more like twilight than afternoon. Had it really turned so much colder, or was it the damp, ominous air?

"The sky's awful," said Maya as they headed for her mother's car. "This storm will be bad."

"Let's skip McDonald's. No sense getting caught on the road home," said Cassie.

"Good idea," Maya's mom agreed. "It's always worse on Northshore Road."

They drove toward the lake. Cassie wondered where on Main Street Diana had met her death. It felt strange to think she'd driven past that spot many times over the years, without knowing the tragedy that had happened there.

All along Northshore Road, dark clouds

threatened the western sky. Out on the water the waves grew fierce and a lone sailboat raced to shore.

Mrs. Bhargavarti turned her headlights on long before they reached Greystones. Cassie said goodbye and ran up the walk. By this time, not a branch moved. No bird sang. Everything was dead still, in that expectant calm before a storm. The air around her felt like something huge, wet and heavy. Crouching, ready.

The front hall was silent and dark. From somewhere on the left came the soft sound of classical music. Reading about her family had reminded Cassie where she could find more information. She walked straight to the library, a room made gloomy by the deep burgundy Persian carpet and walls of dark-bound books.

It didn't take long to find it. The ancient family Bible was thick, and bound with black leather. Cassie carried it to the desk. Too tense to sit down, she opened the book. On the inside front pages, the Denning family tree was recorded in many styles of writing and several shades of ink.

There was her own name, with Dan and Becky and her parents. Beside it, her date of birth was printed in Grandma Denning's precise hand. She looked at the blank spot where someday someone would record her date of death, and shivered.

Diana's name and dates were only one line above hers. Poor Diana.

Carefully she searched through the rest of the chart of Dennings. Outside the wind started again. It whined through the trees, until the pale undersides of the leaves quivered against the dark clouded sky.

Inside, the room turned cold.

As soon as she saw the black lines on the page, Cassie knew she had found it. The angry strokes obviously covered a name — someone with two brothers and a sister. Someone whose parents were Edward and Ruth. Someone who had done something so horrible that her name had been obliterated from her family's Bible.

The soft scent of roses seeped toward her as Cassie turned the page and held it up to the light to see if she could decipher it from the back. No luck. She examined the page itself more closely. In thin tiny letters below the bold strokes was a name. *Catherine Rose Denning, born June 28, 1879.* So someone had still loved Catherine, timidly.

The sky finally opened with a crash, releasing its torrents of hard rain.

It wasn't a sound, but an instinct that made Cassie look up. Across the desk from her stood a girl. Golden-red hair cascaded past her shoulders.

It was the girl in the picture. The girl in the Bible. Catherine Rose Denning, born in 1879.

CHAPTER 12

Cassie stood spellbound, too amazed to react. She could only stare at her shimmering double, tall and thin in a long pale gown. That wild golden hair framed the face once so lovely, but now bleached of life. None of the vitality in the portrait remained.

Except in the eyes. They were too large and dark and hypnotic; too deeply, unnaturally set into her face. So much disdain glowed from them that Cassie stepped back. She felt a scream building up, but suppressed it. This was the one responsible for Cassie's ruined date, her exhaustion and headaches, her fear. Within her, terror fought with anger. But Cassie choked back her rising feelings and forced her voice to be gentle.

"I know who you are, Catherine Rose. Why are you here?"

The room felt ice cold. The scent of old roses had become nauseating. Slowly the girl lifted a thin arm and pointed a finger at Cassie. Her mouth began to move.

Cassie could not tell if she heard or sensed the words, but they echoed, as if spoken in a large empty chamber. "I belong here." Her tone implied that Cassie didn't.

Cassie clenched her hands into tight fists to force herself to stay calm. Think. Find out what she wants, she ordered herself. "Wh . . . what do you want? What are you looking for?"

The ghost became livelier. She moved in an eerie pantomime, swaying rhythmically, as if to music only she could hear. Cassie's mind filled with pictures of gaiety, the ballroom brilliant with light, gentlemen lining up to dance with the belle of the ball.

The ghost was smiling now, a hideous toothy grimace. "To dance. Oh how I long to dance."

It was horrible. Cassie could almost hear the music Catherine yearned for. She steeled herself to stay encouraging. "It sounds . . . wonderful, Catherine."

The ghost of Catherine stopped swaying. Her ruined face twisted. A wave of anger and frustration surged toward Cassie, so strong she reached for the back of a chair to steady herself.

"But I am forbidden . . . A lady must behave with decorum." She stamped a thin slipper-clad foot. "I detest stitching miles of tedious needlepoint, reading the Scriptures for hours, tinkling dull melodies on the piano. It bores me."

For a moment Cassie forgot her terror and felt only sympathy. "I can't blame you," she whispered.

As if she had been slapped, the ghost flinched. She glared at Cassie with scorn. Her paleness turned almost translucent, and her eyes glowed fiercely in the dim, cold room. "No, you are like them. Meek. Self-righteous. Secretly envious."

Cassie's fear returned. It left her in no state to argue. She stood quietly, waiting.

The ghost whined in an echoing whisper. "They lock me in . . . I escape through my window . . . to meet my beaux." She gave Cassie a sly look. "On the shore . . . in the moonlight."

"That's really brave," Cassie said. And desperate, she thought. She imagined Catherine climbing out of a window with one hand, the other holding back her long stiff dress, then sliding to the ground and running lightly, triumphantly, across a dark lawn. "I want to laugh . . . to dance . . . " the ghost almost begged.

Cassie nodded sympathetically.

In a flash the spectre's mood changed. "You're — as dull as the other one!" She spit the words at Cassie. "You waste — " She shuddered and paused.

Had the outburst been too much? Was she fading? I must keep her talking, Cassie thought. I must know what she wants from me.

"Waste what?" Cassie asked.

"Life!" the voice was almost a sob. Beneath the

thin skin, Cassie could almost see each brittle bone. She swallowed a scream.

"I want . . . " The shimmering figure gasped in exhaustion. It darkened and the withered mouth seemed to pout. It whispered harshly, "I was cheated. So I borrow yours . . . "

"Who cheated you, Catherine?" Cassie's voice was also a harsh whisper, her mouth dry from fear. This was it, the moment of truth.

The ghost stood shaking for a moment, her bony hands clawing at the sides of her gown. Then she cried, "My father!" Suddenly her whole thin body heaved and she began to sob. Her anguish filled the room. "My self-righteous father . . . so angry . . . my only chance to get away . . . I ran . . . "

The shrill ring of the telephone on the desk between them pierced the room. Cassie jerked. The ghost moaned and vanished instantly.

The phone shrilled again.

Cassie shook uncontrollably. She pulled the quilt from the couch around herself and sat down, stunned. She thought she would never be warm again.

The phone rang a third time. It didn't occur to her to answer it.

"Telephone for you." Her father said, stepping into the doorway.

Cassie felt too dazed to comprehend the message. "Phone? I — I can't talk now."

Her father looked at her deathly white face, then

at the quilt. He quickly picked up the receiver and said, "Dorian? I'm sorry, Cassie can't come to the phone now. She's not well."

He hung up abruptly and rushed to his daughter. "Cassie, what's wrong?"

She was so shaken she could barely talk. "I'll — I'll be okay."

"We'll see what your mother says when she gets home. Do you need something? I could bring you some Aspirin, or . . . ?"

Cassie huddled on the couch, clutching the bright quilt tightly around herself as if it could defend her from evil. "No, I don't need anything. I . . . "

"Why don't you go to bed? You look totally wiped out."

She shook her head. "Maybe later."

He stood for awhile and watched her helplessly. "Well, if you're sure you don't need me . . . I've got a lot of work to do. Call me if you need anything?"

"Thanks, Dad."

She hunched the quilt up around her shoulders. Go to bed? That was the last thing she'd do. She had to think. *Oh, how I long to dance,* Catherine had said. *I was cheated, so I borrow yours . . .* Cassie thought of the nights when she had woken up more tired than when she had gone to bed. Mornings followed by days of sly looks, rumours, wolf whistles. Had Catherine somehow borrowed Cassie's — what? her energy? her life force? — and used it to

110

go dancing? The idea seemed way too far out, yet it explained a lot.

But this isn't her life — it's *mine*, Cassie thought. I don't want to feel exhausted all the time just so she can party. I don't want to wreck my reputation, my dates with Dorian . . . Dorian! He had phoned. Even after last night's disaster, he still wanted to talk to her. Should she call him back?

She heard the crunch of gravel in the driveway and looked up. A sporty white car sped up the driveway, spraying water in all directions. Mother. Now they'd have to settle last night. Cassie wished it were tomorrow already, with the hassle behind her.

She's taking her time coming, Cassie thought, as she sat waiting, feeling like a mouse who knows the cat is only one leap away. Finally her mother entered the library. Her hair hung damp, but her cool, perfectly made-up eyes studied Cassie hunched miserably on the couch. "Why on earth didn't you tell me you had a date with Dorian Gzowski?"

She never wastes any time on preliminaries, thought Cassie. Looking down at her quilt she mumbled, "I forgot."

"You forgot? Am I that unimportant? Does it ever occur to you that I care about you?"

Cassie was too drained to argue. She shrugged deeper into her quilt.

"Stop that!" commanded her mother. "Talk to me. Tell me what's going on with you."

"Why, so you can tell me how to do it better?"

By the hurt look in her mother's eyes, Cassie knew she'd struck a raw nerve, and felt sorry. She knew her mother's first husband had left her, and she often argued with her sister, so Cassie suspected this accusation had been flung at her before.

What should she say now? She could think only of the creature she had just faced. She could see the pale hollow features and the eyes glowing with envy even now.

Outside the rain sloshed over the eavestroughs and flooded the garden. The wind raged. Cassie hunched further into her quilt, shivering.

"Listen to me, Cassie," her mother said. "At least Dorian is a decent boy and I know his family. He came to the house to pick you up. But who are the others? Where are you meeting them?"

"Others . . . ? What others?" Cassie answered wearily. She knew what was coming.

"Why do you have to hide it from us? Is there something wrong with them?"

"Hide what?"

"You know very well. You've swung from one extreme to the other. First I can't get you to meet new friends. Now I hear some of my nurses have seen you out dancing and carrying on with all sorts of fellows."

Cassie was still too drained to protest with conviction. Hugging her quilt she whispered, "And you believe that?"

"Why would my nurses lie to me?"

"Why would your own daughter lie to you? You *know* me."

"Not anymore. You're behaving so strangely lately, and not telling me anything."

"I've told you everything. I'm *not* wandering around the house at night, and I'm *not* dancing all over town." Cassie stood up. She was so very tired. Letting the quilt drop from her shoulders, she stepped over its limp form and walked out of the library.

As Ellen Denning gaped in surprise, Cassie walked down the hall as if in a trance, opened the front door and went outside. The door swung shut behind her with a finality that made her mother shudder.

The cool wind slapping rain across Cassie's cheeks felt almost good. She walked down the driveway and out along Northshore Road. Soon it was less gloomy than it had been earlier, and the rain had almost stopped. The wild weather made her feel alive and free from everything at home. She wished she could walk out here forever.

Ten minutes later, before she even realized where she was, she reached the sagging iron gates of the cemetery. On impulse, she pushed them open and followed the path to the section where the Denning family lay buried.

She stopped in front of the stones naming her ancestors. The cold marble stood guard over so many stories. Wild Uncle George, buried beside all three of his wives; the love story that had been Grandma and Grandpa, still holding hands at eighty-four and dying within six months of each other; three little Denning sisters wiped out by some epidemic before any of them could reach ten years. Beside them lay Diana's grave. Carved into the white marble was "Our angel waits for us." Cassie ran her finger over the letters.

But it was another grave she really wanted to find. She walked around and carefully studied each headstone. Finally she found the crumbling old stones that covered the resting places of Catherine's family. She read the names, expecting the scent of roses or the familiar chill to assault her. Nothing. She read them again. The gravestone she needed to see was not there.

She searched the other grave sites nearby. To the right she looked until the row ended at the edge of the cliff. On the left she passed the bare patch of grass where she knew she would one day bury her parents. It occurred to her that one day, some future relatives would follow this same path during *her* funeral. It wasn't just the drizzle wetting her cheeks now.

Cassie stared blindly at stones that couldn't possibly be what she was looking for. Where was

Catherine's grave? It wasn't here. Catherine wasn't buried here.

Then where was she?

CHAPTER 13

The sky had darkened again and the drizzle returned to rain as Cassie walked home along the Northshore Road. Only the cries of seagulls broke the silence along this lonely stretch. It suited her mood. She ignored the unfamiliar black Jaguar speeding toward her until it slowed. When it stopped across from her, she hurried on nervously.

"Cassie."

She looked up in relief. Ben's voice. Mr. Straker must have bought another new car.

"Come on. I'll drive you home."

She crossed the road and got into the car. She sat cold, silent and miserable as Ben turned the car around, back toward Greystones. At her driveway, Ben wheeled in and pulled to a stop.

"You're having a rough time of it, aren't you?" His dark eyes looked concerned.

Cassie nodded, and shivered. Ben turned on the

car heater. "Want to tell me about it?"

"I can't unload all this stuff on you. It's too far out."

"Hey, Cass, unload. We haven't gone through years of stuff together to stop now. Remember when you wouldn't tell your parents that it was me who wrecked your bike?"

Cassie tried to smile. "And the time our raft sunk in the lake after we promised we wouldn't go out there?"

"And the year it bothered me so much not to have a dad? You offered to share yours with me."

She was still shaking. Ben took off his jacket and wrapped it gently around her shoulders. "You can tell me, Cassie."

The words rushed and tumbled out of her, "I'm not the dancer . . . a ghost . . . she's awful . . . Catherine . . . uses me . . . the library . . . "

Ben asked her a few questions, then whistled softly. "Cassie, this is tough to believe. This stuff is only supposed to happen in movies."

"I wish it was a movie, so I could just turn it off. It's awful, Ben, and so scary. But it's the truth." She looked at him. "We've known each other for years. Can you believe me?"

"Yes," he murmured, then was silent for a while. "What are you doing out here so late, anyway?" he asked.

"Getting away from my mother. But also . . . " She explained about the graves. "I can't find

Catherine's, Ben. Why wouldn't she be buried with the rest of her family?"

Ben gazed thoughtfully out into the dark. Finally he said, "Maybe she married and moved away somewhere else. Or maybe she died in disgrace. Didn't they used to bury those people outside the holy grounds? At the nearest crossroads or something like that?"

"That's suicides, I think. If Catherine wants so much to be alive now, so much that she's trying to use my life, I can't imagine she wanted to die then. . . She seemed to blame her father for something, though. Do you suppose he — he murdered her, and that's why she's haunting me?"

"Ghosts *are* supposed to return to seek justice. But she doesn't need you to seek revenge on a man who already died ages ago."

"You're right. And anyway, she didn't act like a murder victim. More like a spoiled kid."

"It has to be something else. Something that's still important." The rain pelted the car roof and slapped the windows. "Are you warm enough now?" Ben asked.

Cassie hugged Ben's coat to herself and nodded. "She's only interested in dancing. Forget that vengeance stuff. This girl just wants a good time — no matter what it costs anyone else."

"Which doesn't explain why you can't find her grave." Ben glanced at the dashboard clock. "Listen, I have to pick up some guests of the Strakers from the airport. I'll be late meeting their flight. Cassie, I'm really sorry, but I've got to go."

"Oh. I'm sorry. You go ahead."

"You going to be okay? I wish I could help more," he said as he continued up the drive and stopped by her door.

She pulled off his jacket. "You helped a lot by listening . . . and mostly just by believing me." She handed the jacket over.

He reached out to take it, then ignored it and touched her cheek. "Don't give up, Cass," he said. "We'll figure something out." He leaned over and kissed her.

For a moment she felt so warm and safe she wished the kiss would last forever. But it was over quickly.

"Your parents must be worried, and I'm late." Ben's voice sounded almost gruff.

"Thanks, Ben," was all she could manage to say. She dropped his jacket on the seat and ran up her front steps.

At the front door she paused. Would there be another scene? She dreaded going in.

The front hall was empty. At the living room door, her dad called a cheerful hello, but her mother glared at her with a look she probably saved for viruses. With a quick good night, Cassie headed for bed. She'd gone through more than her share of emotions today. She'd had enough.

She fell asleep with her mind whirling with

images of a hollow-eyed ghost, a tender kiss and a missing grave.

Ben acted the same as always on the bus Monday morning. Cassie was glad, because even though she had thought a lot about yesterday's kiss, it was his friendship she needed now. Besides, she didn't know how to deal with him any other way.

Dorian wasn't on the bus at all, but he was the first person she saw as she entered her History class. He smiled one of his heart-stopper smiles at her, and for a second she thought he would come over. Instead, he took a seat on the other side of the room. She spent the period trying not to stare at him, thinking about the way his hair curled on damp days and wondering if he'd ever bother with her again.

After class, though, he stood waiting for her in the hall. "You were sick this weekend?" He looked almost hopeful, as if that would explain her strange behaviour during their date.

"You wouldn't believe how awful I felt." That wasn't a lie. "I'm better now." That was.

"The flu gets you like that. You probably already had it on Saturday."

"Probably."

He hesitated, then spoke quickly. "Ian MacDougall's having a big birthday party at the golf club in two weeks. Dinner and dancing. Will you go with me? You should be well enough by then."

Cassie prayed she would be. "Two weeks?" She smiled. "I'd like that."

"Lucky Dorian," Mark drawled, as he brushed past them and headed back to his cronies across the hall. Dorian glared at him, but nothing could erase Mark's smirk.

"Catherine's been at it again," Cassie groaned before she realized it.

Dorian looked at her oddly. To cover up, Cassie asked, "Is there some new rumour circulating?"

"I'm sure it's only the product of the fertile compost he calls his brain," said Dorian. Then he looked at her closely. "Cassie? There's more to it than that, isn't there?"

Cassie stared at him, considering. Dorian looked away. Was he trying to spare her — or himself? He looked back at her, and swallowed.

"Is there — do you want to talk about it?"

She hesitated. "No . . . not yet, Dorian." His face looked puzzled. "It's too weird. I barely believe it myself."

"Well, when you're ready." His tone sounded too light. Was he hurt, or relieved?

"Dorian . . . " Cassie was about to try to say more, when a group of others joined them. They asked Dorian about the last soccer game, but they watched Cassie. Some slyly, others with speculation. Cassie realized she'd forgotten to go to the game to take pictures. How would she explain that at tomorrow's yearbook meeting?

The rest of her morning at school couldn't have been worse. As the teacher handed back her weekly French test, he shook his head. She had failed it. No wonder. She couldn't study anymore.

Whenever she came near a group, conversations stopped. One girl made a point of avoiding her. A couple of guys she'd never bothered to notice trailed around after her.

"Hey Catherine . . . " One was nervy enough to grab her around the waist.

She quickly sidestepped his grasp and spoke in her coldest tone, "Wrong girl, buddy. I'm Cassie, not Catherine."

Daunted but not convinced, he shrugged and walked away.

At lunch, she couldn't face the cafeteria. Without waiting for Maya, she bought a bag of chips and walked across the sports field and under the maple trees. This time the trees stood brown and dreary. The sky was grey. She tried to swallow the dry salty chips, but it was too hard.

The next Friday evening Cassie was at her usual job, baby-sitting at the Lambertinis'. Mrs. Lambertini hired her regularly because she trusted Cassie to be able to handle Meggie's asthma. Cassie really enjoyed four-year-old Meggie and her baby brother. "Someday I'd like to have a little girl just like you," she'd once told Meggie as they brushed each other's hair.

The children had been tucked into bed over an hour ago. Cassie dozed on the couch in front of the TV. She hardly heard it. A vicious headache and a distant, steady wailing woke her up.

She bolted upright. What was that noise? Crying. Meggie! Cassie heard her harsh coughing and sobbing. She raced up the stairs to Meggie's room. She grabbed the inhaler, helped Meggie with it until her breathing became steady, and then comforted her until she fell asleep again. Cassie sat by Meggie's bed and watched her for a long time, then checked on the baby and went back downstairs.

Again she dozed off on the couch. Again she was awakened abruptly, this time by the slam of the front door. Mrs. Lambertini was almost sobbing, and Dr. Lambertini was calling her name roughly.

"Cassie? Is anyone here?"

Is anyone here? Cassie rubbed her eyes. Where did he think she'd be? She shook her head to wake up more quickly.

"Aha. You *are* here." Dr. Lambertini said it as an accusation.

"How could you? And I trusted you!" Mrs. Lambertini rushed toward Cassie, her arm upraised as if she were going to hit something.

"Could I what? What's wrong?"

"As if you didn't know! You sneak," cried Mrs. Lambertini.

Dr. Lambertini stared at her and shook his head.

"What have I done wrong? Please. Tell me," Cassie begged. *Now* what had Catherine done?

"You went out! I trusted you with my babies' lives and you left them here alone."

"Out?" If only she could get rid of this pounding headache, she could think clearly. "I was right here all evening."

"Then how do you explain your shoes?"

Cassie looked down at her stocking feet.

"They're by the front door, all wet and muddy. You went out."

"Of course I did. Meggie left her doll in the sandbox. I went outside to bring it in for her."

"Don't lie! We saw you. You were coming out of that old hotel on Main Street — laughing," Mrs. Lambertini said.

"It wasn't me." Cassie's heart sank. She was tired of denying it. The Lambertinis wouldn't believe her. Nobody did anymore.

"It was you. We saw you clearly. We stopped the car and called your name. You laughed at us, and disappeared in the crowd." Dr. Lambertini frowned. "I can't believe this outrageous behaviour, Cassie. Your parents will — "

He was interrupted by hoarse crying. Meggie stood at the top of the stairs, talking in choking sobs. "Mommy, Mommy. I was crying so long and Cassie didn't come. I couldn't breathe." Mrs. Lambertini raced up the stairs sobbing, "Meggie, my baby, Mommy's coming." She clutched the little girl in both arms, stopped and glared down at Cassie.

"I hope I never see you again," she said, and carried her weeping child down the hall.

Cassie had never felt so desperate. She turned toward Dr. Lambertini and begged him to believe her. "I've been here all evening. I did not leave. I wouldn't do that."

He regarded her stonily. "I'll drive you home."

"No, thank you. I can walk."

"It's my responsibility to get you home," he answered, in a tone that implied he was the only one behaving responsibly.

"No. I'll walk." She held her head up with dignity — she hoped — and walked out, carefully shutting the door behind her, even though she wanted to slam it hard enough to crack it. Not until she got to the road did she remember her coat.

"I'm not going back there to get it," she growled at the dark road. She started to run. For the second time that week she hurried down Northshore Road in the dark, crying. And it was all Catherine's fault.

How much damage had the ghost done this time? Too much. Given her a reputation at school. That was bad enough. Then some nurses from the hospital had seen her out with strange boys. Now Dr. Lambertini, who worked with her mother every day, and with Dorian's father, thought she'd sneaked away from her job. Mrs. Lambertini knew everyone in town. Cassie's baby-sitting career was destroyed. And until she could drive, that was her only way to earn extra money.

Cassie shivered and rubbed her arms. Her parents would go ballistic. What would they say? But what could she do about it anyway? She wished she weren't always so tired lately. She couldn't even think straight anymore.

Headlights broke the darkness behind her. She should have moved to the side, but she deliberately kept walking right where she was. She didn't care.

The car raced toward her, swerved sharply, blared its horn and sped into the night. As Cassie felt it tear past, an image flashed into her mind: a girl lying on the road, broken and dead. Near her body stood a truck, and a driver wringing his hands in shock. The image was so terribly clear that she cringed.

"Diana!" she whispered.

Was that what had happened to Diana? Had something — someone — made her life so desperate that she didn't care whether she lived? Had Diana seen what Cassie had seen, felt the way Cassie was feeling? Always to blame, never being believed?

Cassie walked on, slowly. Yes, she remembered now — the ghost had referred to "you and the other one." Was it *Diana* she had meant? Cassie shivered, rubbing her arms and huddling deeper into her sweater. She quickened her step. Somehow, she had stumbled onto a vital clue. She felt it in her bones, and for the first time in a long time, she felt the stirrings of hope. She needed to think, to plan. But first, she needed facts. And there was only one person who could provide them.

No more kid gloves, Dad, Cassie decided. Tomorrow, you are going to tell me *everything* about Diana.

CHAPTER 14

When she woke up the next morning, Cassie didn't need the lingering scent of roses to know Catherine had been in her room. She could feel it.

Her room — her beautiful, comfortable, clean sanctuary — had been invaded.

Her hairbrush and jewellery box had been moved. A dresser drawer was not quite closed. She had a vivid mental picture of Catherine leafing through her magazines, touching the clothes in her closet, examining her CD collection, laughing at her carefully framed photographs.

Cassie felt dirty, violated. She thought of those cadaverous cold hands touching her drawer handles and doorknobs, her clothes, her personal things. She wanted to toss them all out, burn them, or at least scrub them forever.

Throwing off her covers, she jumped out of bed, furious. What gave Catherine this awful power to invade her privacy and her life whenever she wished?

She slammed her magazines and hairbrush into the wicker wastepaper basket. A glint of gold inside it caught her eye. Reaching down, she found Diana's golden locket. She picked it up, brushed it off tenderly, and tucked it under her pillow. Having it there sharpened her resolve to get to the bottom of this.

She stormed to her closet and began to throw her clothes into a laundry heap at the door. Just as the last pair of pants flew through the air toward the pile, her mother walked in. The flying jeans hit Dr. Denning's right leg, slid down, and slumped at her feet.

Mother and daughter faced each other as fury crackled between them. Cassie was glad to be so angry. It made her feel strong enough to stand up to her mother.

"What has got into you? Are you insane?"

Cassie glared. She had never heard her mother shout like that before.

"I've excused your recent odd behaviour, thinking you were passing through a difficult stage. But now you've gone too far!"

Her words hit Cassie like a slap. She yelled right back, "I told you, IT'S NOT ME! Why won't you believe me?"

"There's no need to shout, Catherine." Her mother's voice dropped deadly soft. "I left morning rounds at the hospital early, I'm so disturbed."

She dropped Cassie's coat, the one she'd left last night at the Lambertinis', onto the pile of clothes in front of her. "Aldo Lambertini had an incredible story to tell me today. It's all over the hospital. I can't believe it."

"Then don't!"

"What would possess you to do such a thing? It's irresponsible, dishonest. It's dangerous. How could you do this to those children, to the Lambertinis . . . to us?"

"Mother. You should know me better than that. I did not leave that house. I swear it."

Her mother wavered, doubt and relief filling her grey eyes. Then she said, "But the Lambertinis saw you. They said you turned around when they called your name. How do you explain that?"

"Mother, it wasn't me. It was . . . "

"Who? Tell me. Please."

Cassie ran all the possible answers through her mind. How could she explain it?

"I'm waiting."

Cassie looked at her mother. Her eyes had gone steel hard. Her mouth was a thin tight line. Cassie's heart pounded and her body shook with frustration, but her mouth wouldn't work.

"You can't even answer me. You're unbelievable!" Cassie's mother shouted, and stepped closer toward her.

"Ellen. Cassie. Stop it."

They both turned to the door in surprise. Tom Denning stood hunched in the doorway, his face as old and grey as his sweater. "Anger won't change this, Ellen. It never did," he added, almost to himself. "I've just spoken with Mary Lambertini. She phoned in tears."

He studied each of them. "I knew something was wrong around here. The tension. But this is too much."

"But, Dad — "

"Cassie. Skip the excuses. Even an apology is worthless. If you care for us at all, you must make me a promise. You'll stop this atrocious behaviour now. Before it's too late."

"Dad, let me — "

"Promise!"

"Sure. I promise not to do whatever I haven't done anyway."

"Cassie, take this very seriously."

"You don't know how seriously I'm taking this. I swear, it's not me."

"You've been seen. By friends who have no reason to lie," her mother insisted.

"*I* have no reason to lie. They're making a mistake. It's not me. It's her!"

Cassie's mother groaned with disgust and stormed out of the room. Her father glared at Cassie, but under his anger Cassie saw fear. The despair in his voice made her want to cry.

"Cassie," he said finally, "since the day you were born, I've adored you, enjoyed you, been so proud of you. I prayed you wouldn't change. And now I see it happening again — please, dear daughter, I'm begging you to stop this."

What was he saying? Happening again? And earlier, he had said "before it's too late." Cassie was sure he wasn't just talking about her. He was thinking of Diana. It was time for her to plunge in. She looked him in the eyes and said gently, "Dad, we can solve all this, if you'd answer my questions."

"No. You have to promise me you'll — "

"Dad. I need to know about Diana."

He waited, even paler than before. Cassie blurted her questions quickly, desperately.

"Tell me, please. What was Diana like? How was she acting before she died? Different? Why were you angry with her?" As Cassie talked, she watched her father's face. The sorrow and fear in it told her everything. What was happening to her *had* happened to Diana.

"That has nothing to do with . . ." Her father stopped, unable to go on. He turned to leave the room, then paused and said without looking at her, "I think you'd better not leave the house for anything but school for the next few weeks."

"You mean I'm grounded?" She couldn't be. She had too much to do. "That's not fair!"

"Under the circumstances, it's not only fair, but necessary."

He seemed so weary, so grey. Cassie remembered how happy and carefree he had looked in that sun-filled photo, before he lost his beloved sister.

She could only nod, and turned back to finish cleaning her room.

Later, Cassie phoned Maya. She needed to hear a supportive voice again.

"Hi, Cassie. If you'd hurry up with that driver's licence you could get over here now. Hey, we could even cruise around town a bit."

Driver's licence? Was it only a few weeks ago driving lessons had been her biggest concern? And hadn't she once made a list of all the wonderful things she wanted to do? She didn't even know where it was anymore. "You'll have to be the one, Maya. I stopped thinking about driving lessons. And besides, I'm grounded."

"Grounded!"

"Nice, eh? Sixteen, and I'm grounded like some bratty little kid. Life sure is fair: I'm grounded, I have to cancel next week's date with Dorian, and Catherine gets to dance all over town."

"The phantom struck again?"

Cassie described the baby-sitting disaster. Maya was sympathetic, and added, "Mrs. Lambertini's the worst one you could have picked. She makes such a big deal out of anything to do with her kids."

"You're telling me. What are my chances of ever baby-sitting in this town again?"

"About the same as Brad Pitt proposing to me on TV."

"I can't laugh, Maya."

"Sorry."

"I can't think or sleep or read anymore, either. I'm failing half my tests and my life's a mess. I'm desperate."

"It's getting too serious, Cassie. You have to ask your parents for help."

"I just tried. They didn't exactly come through for me."

"Try again when they're not all riled up."

"How do you explain a ghost to two scientists?"

"Give them scientific information. There are lots of books and studies about it out there. I've been reading so much about ghosts, I'm getting spooked."

"Maya — "

"I'm in the middle of an interesting one now — on possession . . . "

"Possession! You're nuts, Maya."

"Check it out in your history books, Cassie. In the Middle Ages Rome had fifty-two exorcists — all appointed by the Pope — to drive evil spirits out of people. Ethiopians believed in a spirit called *zars*, and European rabbis read the Ninety-first Psalm to get rid of possessing spirits. And — "

"Maya," Cassie broke in, "there's more."

Maya paused. She cleared her throat, then said quietly, "Yes?"

"Catherine has done this before."

"What!"

"Catherine haunted my dad's sister Diana, too. I think that's how Diana died."

"Did he actually say something about it?"

"He can't face it. He admitted Diana started acting strange. But, Maya, listen . . . " Cassie told her his exact words and reactions; shared the ghost's reference to "the other one"; talked about her own feelings last night when she had stayed walking on the road even though she knew the car was coming. As she talked and Maya listened, Cassie felt the beginnings of a plan taking shape in her mind.

"Maya, are you still there?"

"Yeah. Just a little overwhelmed." Maya laughed ruefully. "It's one thing to read about all this in theory, but to actually watch it happen to your best friend . . . "

"You're telling me. Will you do something useful for me?"

"Anything. What?"

"I have to make Catherine go away, and get my old life back. I haven't a clue how to get rid of a ghost who's been around for a hundred years, so I may as well start by clearing myself with my parents and everyone else. Otherwise, even if I do get free of her, no one will believe she ever existed, and I'll be forever guilty. I've got to convince everyone that Catherine is impersonating me."

"Go, girl! That's the old Cassie talking again. But how do you convince them unless they can see both of you at the same time?"

"Exactly. And there are two tricky details. One, I'm grounded. Two, she usually only appears to other people when I'm sleeping, or at least close to sleeping."

"Well, then . . . "

"Stop right there," Cassie laughed. "Seriously, I had planned to spend the night at your place. Invite one or two others over too, to back us up . . . "

"But now you're not allowed out."

"My plan can still work, though."

"Tell me."

"To get a picture of Catherine out dancing. I'll make sure there are witnesses to prove I'm home — "

"Yes! Then I'll photograph Catherine wherever she is. Heck, skip the photos. We'll beat this old ghost the modern way — videotapes. The first to catch a ghost in action. Only one problem."

"I know: Can you really film a ghost?" said Cassie.

"No — I think you can. There seem to be enough photos of them in these books."

"So what's the problem?"

"Where will we find her?" asked Maya.

"She's been at St. Mary's, Beachball's and over in The Blue Lagoon. She wants to dance. Port Morden isn't that big."

"Ben will help. We'll stake out the town together."

"Let me talk to him, Maya. If he can help, I'll ask him to phone you. Talk to you later."

She needed some kindness now, after a morning of yelling and emotions and now Maya's breezy efficiency. As she dialled Ben's number, she thought of the kiss and the comfort with him in the car that night, and of the easy accepting way he always had with her.

Ben still seemed a little dubious about what was causing all of Cassie's trouble, but he quickly agreed to help. "Any idea's a good idea, Cass. At least we'll be taking some action. We'll start tonight."

"Good. My parents are having dinner guests — extra witnesses."

"Leave the legwork to us. Just make sure they notice you all evening, and see you going to bed. Could you get Becky to sleep in your room with you?"

"I'll try to. Um . . . Ben?"

"Yo?"

"Thanks."

"Any time."

Cassie hung up and stood staring out the window for a long time. The warm fall colours had all faded. A few dead leaves still clung to the trees. The bare branches, like hundreds of gnarled fingers, grasped at the grey dreary sky without hope. The last call she had to make — to Dorian — would be the hardest.

The sound of laughter from below startled her from her thoughts. A bright dash of colour — a golden dog and a golden girl in a yellow sweatshirt romped across the lawn. Becky held a stick high and Rumble wagged his tail, barking expectantly. She tossed the stick and they both raced for it.

Cassie smiled to see her sister so lively. There had been some close calls since her birth. Yet it was Becky who gave the laughter and the mischief to the family. It was Becky who slipped walnuts into the dryer, lost her pet garter snake in the kitchen, and ran away from day camp because the games were too boring. Half the neighbourhood had searched for her until she was found cheerfully sharing her lunch with the ducks by the lake. Becky had spunk.

So why did Catherine pick on me? Cassie thought, but immediately squashed the terrible question.

Becky stopped to stroke Rumble and rub noses with him. She saw Cassie at the window and waved. Thank goodness her sister was safe, thought Cassie.

But the question returned, slightly changed. Why choose Diana, for that matter? The locket with Diana's parents' picture inside, her closeness with her younger brother, the tribute in the book — they all indicated someone rather sweet, not Catherine's type either. So what was the connection?

It hit her so physically she was out of breath for a moment before she could run downstairs to the leather Bible in the library.

CHAPTER 15

Cassie shook as she pulled the Bible from the shelf and opened it at the page with the family tree. Quickly she found the entry for Catherine. *Born: June 28, 1879*. She traced her finger down the list of names until she found Diana again. *Born May 14, 1943. Died August 23, 1959*. Then she noticed another ancestor, Victoria. Victoria Denning had died in 1916. April 9. Her birth date was January 11, 1900.

Perhaps it was the round numbers of the turn of the century that made it so obvious. But suddenly that age, sixteen, seared into Cassie's mind. She checked back to Diana's dates — 1943 to 1959. She remembered when the strange things began happening to her — September twentieth. Her sixteenth birthday.

Cassie sat down with the heaviness of the discovery. Somehow, she didn't understand why, some vibration or spirit in the house, or a family curse, enabled Catherine to enter the lives of Denning sixteen-year-olds, and forced them to dance to Catherine's tune.

Cassie looked at the Bible again. May to August. January to April. They hadn't lasted long after their birthdays. About three months. Was this the pattern? Cassie wondered. It was almost November. She'd been sixteen for five weeks now. Time was running out, faster than she thought.

Cassie sprang from her chair and paced the room like a caged wildcat. I have less than two months left? Two months to find out how to get rid of Catherine and do it. Because . . . she stopped by the window. The afternoon sun pierced through the clouds to light the spot where her laughing sister now sat in the grass with her arm around Rumble.

Because if I die, Catherine won't stop. Ghosts go on forever. She'll just wait for the next girl . . . Becky!

Cassie felt sick. In four years she would be long buried in the graveyard down the road, and her sister would become the ghost's next victim. She couldn't let that happen. She had to stop this ghost. But how? No one had believed Diana. Probably not Victoria. Certainly not her.

With these desperate thoughts, Cassie paced the room again. She re-examined the family tree, flipped through the Bible, glared at the richly bound volumes surrounding her, as if they hid the explanation she needed. What about this old house? It had witnessed a century of Denning secrets. Perched high on the top of the cliff, overlooking the land and the lake, did it know the answer?

She was almost relieved when her mother called her to help prepare for the dinner party. They worked together shredding romaine lettuce, chopping almonds, fussing over appetizers, but they might as well have been in separate towns. Her mother worked quickly, quietly. Cassie felt too shaken and overwhelmed by danger to concentrate. She dropped spoons, spilled vinegar, slammed a cupboard door too hard. She knew it was time to get help from her parents.

Her mother looked homey in her apron, stirring here, tasting there. Maybe now was a good time to tell her. The first time Cassie began, the phone rang, and her mother dashed to answer.

The second time, they stood side by side, making dessert. Cassie rehearsed her lines and took a deep breath. She leaned her hand on the counter — and crushed an egg.

Her mother glared at her coldly. "Is this carelessness because you resent having to stay home? Control yourself, young lady."

Cassie watched the egg yolk slide to the floor, and her confidence with it. She'd tell her mother later. When she had the video. The more she thought, the more important that video became.

It would prove her innocence. Once she had concrete proof to show her parents, it would be easier to talk. Then together, they'd figure out how to beat this ghost and live normally again.

Cassie had planned to make sure her parents and their dinner guests saw her every few minutes, bright and cheerful and entertaining, so that they'd notice when she went up to bed. But as the evening progressed, she grew so tired she could barely walk. In between dragging herself out of the kitchen to serve the courses and clear the table, she drank mugs of strong black coffee. Once, she found herself napping in a kitchen chair, so she went to the sink, splashed cold water on her face and rushed to the dining room to offer more coffee.

All the while she thought of Ben and Maya. Talk about Mission Impossible: To search the hot spots of Port Morden with a video camera to film a dancing ghost.

To give them more time, she said good night to her parents and guests and headed up to bed earlier than usual, at ten o'clock.

"I've got some new magazines," she said to Becky. "Want to come to my room and read them with me? Try out some of the hairstyles? We'll have a sleepover."

Becky brought up chips, fudge and pop, and they sat on Cassie's bed, flipping through magazines and munching. Finally, wondering how Maya and

Ben were doing in town, Cassie yawned, said good night to Becky, and fell asleep.

The shrill ringing of the telephone woke her up Sunday morning. She noticed Becky was already gone, but her chips and mess spilled from the bed onto the floor. The phone rang again. Cassie sat up, her heart pounding. She grabbed the receiver.

"We got it! Cassie, we did it!" Maya screeched with excitement.

For a moment Cassie closed her eyes and said a silent prayer of gratitude.

"We didn't want her to see, so we had to film her from across the room, but we got two minutes. Two glorious minutes of Catherine on video. She's walking, she's dancing, she's ours. Cassie, do you know what this means?"

Did she know what this meant? Cassie was overwhelmed by what it meant — her first victory over Catherine. It meant everything. "Come over, Maya. Bring it to me now." Her voice was a barely audible croak.

Within forty minutes Maya, Ben and Cassie stood in Cassie's family room, watching the video of Catherine Rose Denning, born 1879 yet not looking a day over sixteen, dancing to a modern rock song. She glowed with vitality and happiness. The enormity of it awed them.

When it ended, Cassie had tears in her eyes. Ben took the video from the machine and presented it gravely to her. She reached for both friends in a hug. "I can't thank you enough. You've saved me."

Maya stood misty-eyed and speechless beside her, until Ben said, "Call your parents, Cass. It's time to get into high gear."

Cassie ran to the kitchen where her father had been brewing coffee awhile ago. He must have already taken it to his office. Her mother was upstairs. Cassie put the video down and hurried to find her parents.

The Dennings followed their wild-eyed daughter, unable to comprehend what she wanted, but sensing her urgency. They entered the kitchen where Becky was cooking oatmeal in the microwave.

"You come watch this too, Becky," Cassie said triumphantly, heading for the table where she had dropped the tape.

It was gone.

Cassie was afraid to breathe.

Her mother sniffed the air. "What's that smell in here? Cheap rose perfume?"

"Maya! Ben!" Cassie screamed. "Did you take the video?"

Her friends rushed to the kitchen looking puzzled. Becky opened the microwave and took out her oatmeal. "Is this it?" she asked. "Your tape's right here, on top of the microwave."

Cassie was relieved, until she saw Maya's face.

Maya looked sick. "The microwave? Omigod."

She snatched the film and ran with it to the family room. The others followed her in confusion.

Cassie could barely breathe. Had it been too good to be true?

With shaking hands, Maya slipped the video into the machine and turned it on. The screen flickered into light. It crackled and hummed. Everyone watched and waited.

The music, Catherine's rock music, began. Cassie looked at her parents standing by the couch, watching the TV expectantly. In a few seconds, they would finally believe her. She couldn't stand the suspense another moment.

With a loud hiss, a picture flashed on. It flickered green and red and jagged, poison yellow. Black spikes streaked through it. Finally, the screen focussed on people, then flipped and lurched into waves. Now and then a face wobbled into view, only to drift away before it could be recognized.

Cassie wanted to throw up. She felt completely crushed. Maya and Ben looked stunned.

"Great movie, guys. It looks like the waves of colour are dancing to the beat of the music. I like it." Becky laughed and went back to the kitchen.

Cassie's dad shuffled impatiently, and her mother checked her watch.

"But we had it," Cassie protested. "I'll rewind it. We'll put it in slow motion. Wait. We'll make it work." She pushed buttons and dials, pulled the video in and out, tried fast forward and rewind. She had to keep moving or she'd break down. She had counted on this film so badly.

"I have work to do upstairs. Call me if you get it fixed," Ellen Denning said abruptly and walked out.

Seeing his daughter's distress, Tom Denning helped her adjust some dials. "What was it about?" he asked kindly.

The weight of disappointment on top of everything that had happened this weekend crushed Cassie's hopes. She knew she couldn't convince her dad that this jagged video had shown a dancing ghost. Already he didn't trust her. She'd only make it worse if she tried. "It wasn't important, Dad. It was a stupid idea . . . "

"No, it was a good idea," Ben interrupted. "We were going to show you — "

"The girl who looks like Cassie," cut in Maya smoothly. "It's too bad the tape got fried by the microwave."

Cassie's father frowned. "Cassie, did you put them up to this?" He looked at Maya and Ben. "Look, your loyalty to your friend is commendable, but it's misdirected. Instead of coming up with some story about a girl no one else can see, why don't you convince her to start behaving normally again? Then you'd really help her." With a frown at Cassie, he turned and stalked out of the room.

"Well, that sure convinced him. You must be glad you went to all that trouble for me." Cassie flopped down onto a chair. "Oh, what's the use."

Maya spoke. "Cassie. We're so close. Don't give up now. We'll do it again. Next time it will work."

"No, it won't. She'll find some other way to wreck it."

"You can't think that way," said Ben. "We'll film her again, and we won't let the tape out of our hands. We'll bring it over the minute we get it, even if it's really late by the time we get here."

Cassie stared at Ben. "What do you mean, really late? What time did you actually see Catherine last night?"

"What was it — nine-fifteen, nine-thirty?" Ben looked at Maya and she nodded.

"But. . . I was still awake at nine-thirty," said Cassie. "Dead tired, but awake. I didn't even go upstairs until ten."

The three looked at each other in dismay.

"She's getting stronger," whispered Cassie. "She's winning."

After Maya and Ben left, Cassie walked slowly across the fields to the cemetery, seeing only gloomy skies and the lake that was even darker.

Before the grey gravestone of Diana, she stopped, too numb to think or pray. At her feet, geraniums drooped brown and limp. By the time they bloom again, she thought, I'll be dead.

CHAPTER 16

Monday morning a cold rain drizzled from a dreary sky. Cassie dragged herself around the school. How could she ever pull her life back together, she wondered, when she felt too tired to care?

She turned a corner and almost bumped into Dorian. "Oh . . . hi." She was nervous, but he looked around as if he were trapped.

"Uh — hi."

She had to get it over with. "Dorian. About the party . . . " Why wouldn't he even look at her? He kept fidgeting with his books. She couldn't see his face.

"I can't go to Ian's party with you after all. My parents made other plans without telling me."

"That's okay. It happens."

Did he sound relieved? Was he ashamed to be seen dating her? And she had worried so much over what to say to him.

"I'm late, Cassie. See you later." Dorian Gzowski,

the boy she thought she could love a lifetime, hurried down the hall away from her as fast as he could.

Cassie found Maya walking into Math and pulled her by the arm. "Come with me. We have to talk."

In an empty washroom, Maya asked, "Are you all right?"

"No. Look at me!" Cassie gazed at her pale reflection in the mirror. "I've lost weight, there are bags under my eyes, I'm afraid to sleep. I'm a wreck."

Maya nodded sympathetically.

Cassie continued. "I didn't tell you yesterday, but I found someone else."

Maya looked puzzled.

"There was a Victoria. She died almost three months after her sixteenth birthday, just like Diana. And Maya — how old am I?"

Slow realization crossed Maya's face. She trembled, and seemed close to tears. That frightened Cassie even more.

"If I'd known this yesterday, I would have made your parents listen to us. It's . . . " Maya stopped as a girl came in, headed for the mirror, and took her make-up from her purse. Maya brushed her hair, while Cassie rinsed her face with cold water, trying to pull herself together. She looked up in time to see the girl staring at them strangely and Maya sending back a withering look. The other girl rolled her eyes and left the washroom.

Suddenly Cassie felt guilty. "Oh, Maya," she whispered. "I've been so selfish. You're getting hurt by this too."

Maya shrugged. "I'll cope."

"You don't have to. We should stop hanging around together for awhile. I'll understand." Losing her friend would devastate her, but Cassie had to offer. She knew how long it had taken Maya to fit into this tight little community.

"No way. We're friends," Maya declared. "Besides, I know how it feels to be harassed for something that's not your fault," she added softly.

Cassie hugged her. "You're really something."

They headed for classes while Cassie continued their earlier conversation. "I should have told my parents while you and Ben were there to back me up."

"Don't blame yourself. We were all too stunned about the ruined video. Why don't you tell them tonight?"

"What do I say? How can I make them believe me? Especially when my dad doesn't want to."

On the bus home Cassie hunched in her seat, practising her story for her parents. The bus seemed noisier than usual. In front of her, Becky and her friends planned their outfits for the Halloween dance coming up on Friday night. Only one other person looked as quiet and glum as she did.

Dorian stared out the window, miles away from the sound of the other kids around him.

As she walked up the driveway with Becky, Cassie worried about what she'd say. Should she speak to Mother first? Tell them together? No. Dad had always been easier to talk to — less impatient. And on some deeper level, he had to know. He couldn't face it, but he knew. Well, he'd *have* to face it. Tonight, after dinner.

"The house looks dark," Becky groaned. "Blast! I don't feel like starting supper tonight."

Cassie unlocked the back door and saw the note on the kitchen table. It was written in their mother's usual prescription scrawl. *Dad gone to Baltimore — business. I'm in emergency surgery. Will call when able. M.*

Although Cassie was bitterly disappointed, it was Becky who raged. "I'm so sick of macaroni and cheese dinners. We can't even get anyone to deliver a pizza here to the outback. And I wanted Mother to drive me to town to buy the stuff for my Halloween outfit."

Cassie was too depressed to answer. Dinner didn't matter. She'd spent hours psyching herself up for a confrontation with her parents, and now this. She flopped onto a kitchen chair as Becky rummaged around in the fridge.

"I hear living well is the best revenge." Becky grinned and pulled a chocolate mousse cake out of the freezer. She set it in the microwave and poured two glasses of milk.

Cassie watched the microwave timer ticking off the minutes and seconds. Becky filled the silence chattering about school and her plans for the Halloween dance.

For the first time Cassie realized her sister never mentioned the rumours about her. Had the stories not filtered down to Becky's school yet, or was Becky just being kind? Cassie couldn't ask until she was prepared to tell her everything. Someday, very soon, she'd have to warn Becky. But not yet. Not until she could also give her hope.

As Becky sliced the cake, Cassie decided a letter would be best. She'd write down what had happened and what she knew, and give it to Becky — or leave it for her, if it was already too late.

After supper, there was still no word from their parents. Becky went off to do homework, and Cassie phoned Maya.

"How did your parents take it?" Maya asked.

Cassie rubbed her temples. Her head ached. "Dad's gone to Baltimore and Mother's at the hospital."

"Why does their timing have to be so lousy? Why can't anything ever go right?" Maya almost sobbed.

Cassie was taken aback. "Maya. What's wrong?"

"My grandmother — she had a stroke."

"Oh, Maya. I'm so sorry. How bad is it?"

"We're not sure yet," Maya took a deep breath. "Promise me you'll talk to your mother when she gets home. I can't worry about my grandmother and you too."

"Of course I will."

"Your life may depend on this, Cass. If you don't tell her soon, I'll talk to my parents."

"They hardly need this piled on them now."

"They'll understand. Meanwhile, I have another plan." Maya sounded brisk and efficient again. "Maybe we can get through to Catherine. Find out what makes her tick . . . or dance."

"Are you crazy?"

"Probably, but I've been reading about this and we've got nothing to lose. We should try a home circle."

"A home circle? It sounds like a cookies-and-crochet magazine," said Cassie.

"It's sort of like very deep relaxation, but you do it in a group . . . "

"No way. I'm not getting into that weird stuff." Cassie felt so dizzy, she pulled the phone to her bed and lay down. She should have eaten some of the cake.

"You're already into weird stuff — dangerous weird stuff. Do you have a better idea?"

Cassie closed her eyes. "So what's a home circle?"

"We need to get a group together — the right group — that can build up enough psychic power to receive a message from the spiritual dimension."

"Get out," Cassie opened her eyes and laughed. "You, the honours science student, believe that?"

"I believe a spirit is haunting you." She sounded so solemn that Cassie knew she was serious.

"Let me think this over, Maya. The efficient Dr. Denning has to come home some time."

In the school cafeteria on Tuesday, Maya explained the home circle to Ben and Cassie. "See, it's all outlined in this book. It makes sense." She pushed a worn white paperback across the table. "It's like meditation. All we have to do is relax, open our minds. We don't demand facts, don't try to reach out to anything or anyone. All we want to do is be ready to receive whatever we might be given."

"Receive what we're given? Who's going to give us something, Maya?" Cassie was tense. She'd waited up for her mother until eleven-thirty last night, and finally lost the battle to stay awake.

"Whoever, whatever chooses to tell us something. Hopefully Catherine herself."

"Catherine's having a good time. Why would she help me destroy her?" Cassie laughed bitterly. "Diana, Victoria, their parents — they couldn't help themselves, and they can't help me. They're all dead, Maya. Dead and gone."

"Hey, what happened to the girl who used to climb trees and sail Lake Erie on a dare?" Ben asked gently.

"She's gone too." Cassie was shaking so much she spilled her drink.

Ben wiped up the mess with napkins as Maya

spoke urgently. "But Catherine isn't gone. All that passion and desire to get out and have fun — those emotions have held her here. They'll keep her here forever, unless we do something."

Cassie stared at the book. "I don't know. It's just too hard to believe."

Ben touched her shoulder and said, "Thomas Edison, the most brilliant inventor in history, believed it. He figured energy, just like matter, is indestructible. It's all still out there somewhere. He even tried to invent a radio that could pick up sounds of the past."

Cassie felt too weary to answer. How she wished she could just go home and sleep and forget everything. Slowly she cleared away her lunch things.

"Have you talked to your parents yet?" Ben asked.

She closed her eyes. "No. Besides, even if they believed me, they wouldn't know what to do."

As if on cue, the lunch bell rang.

"The longer you wait, the stronger and more dangerous Catherine's ghost becomes. Does that sound better than a home circle?" said Ben. Then, more gently, he added, "I'll see you both at the yearbook meeting," and headed for the door.

Maya watched Dorian leaving the cafeteria ahead of them. "What's wrong with him lately?" she said.

"Beats me. He hasn't talked to me for a week."

"He didn't seem the type to be scared off by rumours."

"Guess he is."

"Well, it obviously bothers him."

"The hottest guy in school doesn't need to worry about me."

"You underestimate yourself, girlfriend."

"Hey, Cassie," a voice interrupted. "There's a big bash at Kyle Peck's this weekend."

Two grade nine guys, looking desperately cool with their nose rings and baggy jeans, stood grinning at them. "Kyle's parents are away. It'll be so good. You two going?"

"Sorry, boys, we don't baby-sit on weekends," Maya answered coldly, and pushed past them.

The girls reached their lockers and dialled their combinations. When Cassie's wouldn't open, she punched it. Maya looked at her in surprise, and quietly turned her lock for her. The door pulled open smoothly.

Cassie ignored the teacher glaring at her and grabbed the books she needed. "I can't believe this is happening. Just this summer I was happy."

"There wasn't a ghost stealing your life this summer." Maya held the white paperback out to her. "If you liked the way it was, you'll have to fight for it."

Cassie snatched the book from her hand. "Okay, okay. I'll read it. I'll talk to my mother. I'll do anything."

Two days later, Maya sat down next to Cassie during study period. Cassie looked up and noticed

Maya's pale face and puffy eyes. "How's your grandmother?" she asked.

"The same. Can't move the left side of her body. My parents leave for India this afternoon. They don't know how long it'll be, so I'm stuck here worrying."

Cassie rubbed her eyes. "You're sure you didn't stay because of me?"

"Yes, I'm sure." Maya frowned. "Another headache?"

Cassie nodded, then winced.

"You haven't told your mother, have you?"

Cassie held her head in both hands, as if that could contain the pain. "I talked to her last night."

"And?"

"She called me to her room. She's worried about my behaviour and the way I look — she thinks it's drugs. I swore it isn't. She seemed relieved, until I tried to tell her about the ghost. That did it. Now she's convinced I'm mentally ill."

"But you're telling the truth. She *has* to trust you."

"She won't. She's always so right and sure of herself, she won't even listen. She's checking out psychiatrists."

"The psychiatrist will believe you."

"Sure, after two years of therapy." Cassie put her aching head down on her desk. "It's just too hard."

"Cassie. Don't give up. Concentrate on your photos, your future, everything good in your life. Think about your sister. Do you want Becky to go through this?"

"Never."

"Then let us help you."

"You mean a home circle. What for?"

"Because it's all we have."

Cassie rubbed her head. It *was* all she had. Becky might have even less.

"Okay, Maya. Let's do it."

"Good. When?"

"When?"

"Set a date, Cassie."

"Friday night? My courage won't last any longer."

"That's Halloween!"

"Why not? All the souls of the dead are supposed to be floating around that night anyway." Cassie gave a hollow laugh.

Maya smiled back. "Friday night it is."

The study bell rang. Maya kept planning as they packed up their books and left the room. "Now, who else can fill the circle? I've thought about this a lot. The book says to choose three or more people who usually meet the same day each week. They already have a sort of harmony." Now that she could use her research and get into action, Maya was all business. She adjusted her glasses and continued. "Your logical choice is Ben and I. We're friends. We meet at the yearbook twice a week, and you two share the bus every day."

"And you're the only ones who believe me."

"It would be better if we had one more person . . ."

"There's no one."

" . . . who we meet with regularly, like on the yearbook staff and the bus."

Cassie stopped walking. "You mean Dorian? He's not even talking to me."

"It would be nice, but we'll manage anyway. Now, in case you don't get around to reading the book, I'll explain a few things to you."

Cassie tried to concentrate on Maya's instructions.

"We'll need a quiet, well-ventilated room. Leave a window open a crack. The seats should be comfortable, and have some water handy. No food or any other drinks though. Oh, and the lights. Keep them low. Can you get candles? Electrical lights set up magnetic vibrations that interfere with communication."

The list dazed Cassie. "We have candles, and storm lanterns. I'll find them. How will I remember all this?"

"Don't worry. I'll handle it. Just keep everything relaxed and quiet."

"Relaxed? How do I relax when my life depends on this?"

Maya looked straight at Cassie, her brown eyes magnified through her glasses — intense and almost hypnotic. "You'll relax *because* your life depends on it. Remember this line: The power of us all, is greater than one."

"The power of us all, is greater than one? I want to believe it, Maya. I do."

"Will your family be home?"

"Becky's going to the school dance, then spending the night at Erin's. Dad's still away, and Mother's on emergency duty again."

"Put Rumble outside in his kennel." Maya briefly took her hand. "This will work, Cassie."

All the way home on the bus, Ben encouraged her too. She could believe him until they reached Greystones, standing stark against the evening sky.

She got off the bus behind Becky and was surprised to see a blue van parked at the entrance to their driveway. The driver's door was open, and beside it, Mrs. Lambertini was pacing nervously.

Cassie was annoyed and worried. She couldn't handle another scene. Now what was wrong?

CHAPTER 17

Cassie stopped beside the blue van, stiff and defensive. Her sister looked at their nervous neighbour, and turned pale. "Is Mother all right?" she asked in a tiny voice.

Mrs. Lambertini looked at her in surprise. "Yes, she's fine, Becky. I came to talk to Cassie."

"Oh." Becky sounded relieved. "I'll go on in. See you later," she called to Cassie, and ran up the driveway.

Cassie waited without speaking.

Mrs. Lambertini pushed her dark hair back, coughed twice, then said hoarsely, "I've come to apologize . . . . We were wrong about you last week . . . "

Cassie was too surprised to answer.

" . . . We should have trusted . . . you were always dependable . . . but we saw someone who . . . " Mrs. Lambertini stumbled so hard for the right words, it was embarrassing.

"It's all right, Mrs. Lambertini. But how did you

find out the truth?" What wonderful miracle had happened? Cassie wondered, her heart racing. Had the ghost given herself away? Would everyone finally believe her?

"It was Dorian."

"Dorian?"

"Dorian Gzowski, my godson. We had dinner with his family last night and . . . " She blushed and coughed again. "We happened to mention that incident."

Cassie could imagine the conversation.

"Dorian explained everything. He said he was on the phone with you that night. He knew the exact time, because he had the radio on. He had no idea who the girl we saw in town was, but he thinks she may be new. Apparently other people are mistaking her for you too."

He lies in convincing detail, thought Cassie. She was absolutely amazed. She hadn't got rid of Catherine yet, but she had gained a new ally.

"Cassie, how can I apologize enough? But why didn't you tell us?"

"You weren't exactly listening," Cassie answered abruptly. She resented that they hadn't believed her when she told the truth, but they'd trusted Dorian's lie.

"I guess we weren't." Mrs. Lambertini blushed again. "How can we make it up to you?"

"You could do me a huge favour," said Cassie. "Please tell my parents what you've found out.

They're really upset about all of this too." She hoped the Lambertinis would do it even half as quickly as they'd spread the bad news.

"Yes, of course we will," Mrs. Lambertini assured her, and offered her hand. "I'm sorry, Cassie. My husband is too. Meggie misses you. When we've all had time . . . Maybe we can try again?"

Cassie hesitated, then shook hands, and forced a polite, neutral answer. But she knew she would never work for the Lambertinis again. Their anger and bitter words that night still hurt.

After Mrs. Lambertini drove away Cassie knew what to do. She walked up Northshore Road to Dorian's house.

It was as if he was waiting for her. He stood out at the mailbox, sorting through some letters, watching her come closer.

"Mrs. Lambertini just apologized to me."

"She should have."

"I don't know why you did it, but thank you. Dorian . . . What if she finds out you lied?"

"She won't. You didn't leave that house."

"You sound certain."

Dorian studied the mail for a moment before he looked at her and answered quietly, "To tell you the truth, for awhile I did wonder."

"I know."

"The stories are everywhere."

Cassie winced.

"I've thought a lot about everything I've known

about you since we started at Lakeside . . . "

He's noticed me that long? Something inside her wanted to smile.

"It didn't add up. You'd never leave Meggie and the baby alone. And you're not some dancing bimbo. It wasn't you the guys saw at Beachball's that night you fell off the dock, and it's not you they've seen since. I don't know who it is — I made that up about a new girl — but I know it's not you."

Cassie wished she had the nerve to hug him. Instead she looked at him and said, "Dorian, are you ready to hear a really weird story?"

Halloween on the lake always lived up to its image. A pale moon cowered behind the clouds, so the night seemed darker, and the shadows closer. The wind from the lake wailed mournfully through the trees, and cold across the lawns. No happy little trick-or-treaters ventured up the few long driveways on Northshore Road. Their parents drove them to town instead.

Cassie had felt chilled and uneasy all day. This morning the portrait of Catherine had fallen again with a crash that echoed down the hall. Was this an omen? She couldn't stand looking at that horrid smiling face anymore, so she stuffed it, face down, into the back of a closet.

Now, even in jeans and a big woollen sweater, she shivered as the four friends sat down in the music room of Greystones. After she had told

Dorian everything, he'd offered to join the home circle. She had gratefully accepted.

Maya, in a long loose dress, her black hair falling free around her dark face and dark eyes, looked exotic and mysterious. As she lit more candles, she gave last-minute instructions.

"No matter what happens, stay calm. Just keep thinking about someone or something that might help Cassie. Notice and remember not just everything you see, but anything you hear, and even what you think." Then she clicked off the light switch.

In the dim, quiet room, Cassie sipped a glass of water nervously, wishing it were coffee. But that wasn't allowed. She smiled nervously at each friend in turn — Maya, Ben and Dorian — and said softly, "The power of us all, is greater than one," as if it were a prayer.

Maya continued softly, "One of us will probably turn out to be stronger than the others. If it's you, and you get a chance to ask questions, don't ask anything that can be answered with just yes or no. Get it to talk longer, to tell us something we don't already know."

Finally, Maya too quietly waited.

In the gloomy room, the four sat. They tried to relax, but the flicker of the candles made grotesque shadows quiver on the walls around them. They looked away and kept waiting.

Dead silence filled the room. They had no idea

how long they sat. Maya had banned even wrist-watches, which might increase the tension, weaken the harmony. So they waited, afraid to look around, and afraid not to.

The room grew chill and a sweet smell of roses made them stiffen with apprehension. The scent seemed to be stronger first here, then there, but they saw nothing. They heard nothing. Cassie knew she would detest roses for the rest of her life.

Then the chill and the smell drifted away, and the room seemed emptier. Maya held her finger to her lips and slowly shook her head. They must continue waiting. Dorian shifted his legs and Ben tried a weak grin. For Cassie, it was an effort even to breathe.

Suddenly she saw a flicker of movement beside the piano. A gasp from nearby told her the others saw it too. Slowly, almost the way an instant photograph got clearer and clearer as it developed, an image appeared. It was a large man, shaking his fist. Cassie cringed, until she noticed that he left no shadow on the wall. Then she sat silently, carefully watching.

The figure was tall, with a proud, aggressive bearing, like a man used to being obeyed. In his right hand he clutched a quill pen. He held it like a dagger, brought it down hard onto a book in front of him, and slashed it across the page.

Cassie would swear later that he then spoke out loud. It was the others who told her the only voice in the room that night was hers. For an instant they had seen a vision of an angry man in an old-fashioned suit. When it had disappeared, they hadn't seen or heard a thing.

The man threw down the pen and shouted, "She is gone. We will never speak of her again. Never!"

As he slammed the book shut, he vanished.

Cassie sat astounded, her heart pounding. He had been so furious. But from his clothes she knew he had lived years ago. Could anger last such a long time?

Then she became aware of another presence in the room. A glimmering shape, like a candle flame just blown out, stood in front of the window. With shock she realized that it was the same person. This time she could see the dark outlines of trees outside, right through him. This time there was no anger, no pride, no power. Just a sad, pathetic old man.

He glanced at her with huge hollow eyes. His face lit up with joy and relief and he began to move toward her. Before she could react, he stopped and shook his head. Cassie was sure she saw tears in his eyes. He looked so heartbroken Cassie wanted to weep for him. Apparently sorrow could last forever too.

She tried to pull herself together. She was here to get information, she reminded herself. To save herself and her sister. Maya said they were to ask questions. What could she ask? She decided to start with something simple. "Who are you?"

The apparition gazed sadly at her. As with Catherine's ghost, she felt, rather than heard, the words he spoke. "Where is she? Find her . . . find her . . . "

Before Cassie could respond, he and the darkness beyond the window became one.

She flopped back in her chair, exhausted, but strangely calm. It was over, and she was disappointed. She wished it had been her father's sister. Diana knew Catherine's awful power. Surely she could have given them some answers, instead of more questions.

She noticed the others watching her curiously, and managed a weak smile. As soon as they saw it, they began to fire questions at her. They had not seen the second figure. In fact, they had been ready to break after the first appearance, until they had seen Cassie's face turn to the window, and heard her speak.

Soon Dorian was making them all coffee, while they exchanged impressions and theories. After a while, their voices began to sound far away and Cassie stopped listening. She remembered instead the sorrowful voice, begging *Find her . . . find her*.

Did he mean Catherine? Was he Catherine's father? Somehow she knew it was. Cassie remembered her own futile trips to the cemetery. She couldn't find Catherine either. And if Catherine's father couldn't find his daughter after a century of searching, how could *she*?

CHAPTER 18

"Why can't I find her?" Cassie repeated to the library walls much later that night. Wearing Dan's yellow sweatshirt over her pyjamas, she sat alone, thinking. It would be dawn in a few hours, but for once she wasn't sleepy. A terrible sense of urgency kept her alert.

Find her . . . Find her. Why? How?

Once the drama of seeing the ghost had ended, the energy had drained from the home circle. The four of them had discussed and tried to interpret the man's words and actions, over and over again, until they realized they were only talking in circles.

Cassie had been relieved when Ben and Dorian finally left. She almost wished Maya weren't staying overnight, except she hated to be alone in the house tonight. Why was her mother so late?

Maya had wanted to organize the next action, to search through ancient photos and confirm that the man in the music room really was Catherine's father. But Cassie needed to be alone. She was glad when Maya finally fell asleep and she could slip downstairs. Here in the silent book-lined room, where a light from the hall provided a small, comforting glow, she could think.

She didn't need old photos. She was certain that the ghost was Catherine's father. Maya had guessed that the reason they had all seen the first apparition was that it represented an event, a flash of emotion so intense it was preserved for eternity. The second figure had been a restless spirit searching for his daughter and pleading for help from one of his descendants. Beyond that Cassie knew no more than she had before.

She gazed around at the walls of books. How ironic, she thought. Here I am surrounded by hundreds of volumes of knowledge, and I don't know anything. But there was a book in that first image. It was important. Is it here now? Which one is it? If this were a movie, she thought wistfully, I'd find an old diary now — with all the answers.

She gazed at the window to the blackness outside. Part of the answer was somewhere out there in the lonely fields, or below the cliff where waves rolled forever to the shore, or beyond. All she could see was the reflection of herself frowning in the glass.

Herself. It always came back to that.

She stiffened. Was it getting cold in here?

No. It was just nighttime in a drafty old house

by the lake. She hugged herself and remembered Catherine's visit to her in this room.

Cassie had been studying a book before that visit. Of course! The Bible. The family tree on its front pages. Cassie switched on a lamp, grabbed the Bible from the shelf and flipped to the chart of the Denning family.

She realized what she had witnessed — Edward Denning had made those angry black strokes that disowned his daughter. Cassie touched the tiny letters timidly declaring Catherine's place in the world. The handwriting looked feminine. *Catherine Rose Denning. Born June 28, 1879.* There had to be a clue here. What was it?

Or was the clue in what was *not* here? There should have been another date, a date for when Catherine died. *There was no record of Catherine's death!*

Cassie thought of the old cemetery down the road, where the lake winds battered the gravestones of all her Denning ancestors — except one. She had searched twice since that stormy evening visit, but she'd never found the grave she wanted. Why not?

Catherine's hollow words echoed through her mind. *My self-righteous father . . . so angry . . . I ran . . .*

Could Catherine's father have killed his own daughter? He'd looked angry enough to. But then he would know where she was — especially if he had buried her secretly to cover up his crime. He wouldn't be wandering through the years, searching for her.

Then Cassie remembered Catherine's other words. *To meet my beaux, on the shore, in the moonlight.* What if Catherine had run away with one of her boyfriends? That would explain why her father had disowned her. He had assumed she'd run away with someone to a life of sin. Perhaps with that scandalous painter. She had disgraced the family name, lost her right to belong. But in all those years her father had forbidden anyone to speak of her, he must have secretly longed to hear from her again. Perhaps he had hoped she would eventually contact him with news of a respectable marriage, contentment, children — his grandchildren. And when no word came, had his last prayer been that they might finally meet in heaven? Then he had been disappointed, for he was still waiting.

Cassie frowned. Where was Catherine? Or rather, where was the mature, forgiving daughter Edward Denning hoped to meet? The only one Cassie had ever seen was a rebellious teenager.

The answer to all her questions crept over her like a cold draft. Somehow, something had gone terribly wrong the night Catherine had escaped for the last time. She had met, not with the beau she expected, but with death. Could she have been murdered by the man she met on the beach? It didn't make sense. Then Catherine's ghost would

have been seeking justice, not good times and dancing. No, it had to be something unexpected, something sudden, catching Catherine alone. For no one
knew she had died. That's why there was no date
in the family Bible, and no grave for Catherine.

A sudden gust of wind outside pushed the
branches against the windowpanes so it sounded
like scratching. It moaned down through the fire-
place and into the room. Cassie glanced around
nervously. Why wasn't her mother home yet?

She went to the front hall and gazed out a
window, over the fields and down the road. There
was only darkness. And somewhere out there,
Catherine — her body undiscovered, her spirit still
wandering around looking for excitement, oblivious to the lives she'd ruined.

Am I supposed to find the body of a girl who died
a century ago? Cassie asked herself. The idea overwhelmed her. No one else in one hundred years had
found her. How could Cassie? Where would she
look? Was there even anything left to find?

Cassie began to pace the hall as Edward Denning's words echoed through her mind. *Find her . . .
Find her . . .*

If I find Catherine and bury her properly, Cassie
thought, not only can Edward Denning rest in
peace — Catherine might too. And I'll be saved.

But if I don't, she'll destroy me.

Headlights glared along the road and turned up
the driveway. Good, her mother was finally coming

home — but not at her normal breakneck speed. Moments later, Ellen Denning walked in the front door, her shoulders hunched.

Cassie had seen her like this before, and greeted her quietly.

Her mother faced Cassie with tired grey eyes. "I'm sorry I'm so late. Had four patients in Emergency — car accident — a family hit by a drunk driver."

She brushed her hands across her eyes. "I thought I could save the boy. I was so close. He was just a kid."

Cassie guided her mother down the hall to the kitchen and pulled out a chair for her.

"His parents had so much faith in me. I couldn't help them, Cassie. I couldn't save him." She covered her face with her hands, while Cassie heated some milk in the microwave.

"I'm sorry, Mother. I know you did your best," she said gently.

"But it wasn't enough." Ellen Denning stopped and stared at nothing. "This is the part of being a doctor that I will never, never get used to."

Cassie handed her a mug of hot milk. She couldn't imagine getting used to it either. "But look how many people you've saved."

"Thank you. Tomorrow I'll keep telling myself that too." She looked down at her slim surgeon's hands. They shook so much they could barely hold the mug. Slowly she spoke. "When I'm with a family like tonight, when I have to tell them the awful news, I'm sick inside. I feel their pain. And when I see their courage, I'm in awe, because I know that if it were me, if I ever lost any of you, I'd fall apart. Nothing in my life would matter anymore."

Cassie looked at her mother, now crying silently, with surprise. She was always so controlled, so superior.

As if reading her daughter's mind, Ellen Denning looked up at her. "I suppose I don't stop to tell you enough how important you are to me."

"Not really."

"And you can't see it yourself?"

"Not when you always tell me how to do everything better." She said it gently. Her mother hurt enough already.

"Cassie . . . I guess I get pretty awful sometimes. You know how much trouble it's caused me."

Cassie nodded.

Her mother took a sip of hot milk, then looked up with tear-smudged eyes. "Why can't we just get along, Cassie? Why can't you like me?"

"Me like you? You're worried about me liking you?" She was amazed. "It's more the other way around."

"Is that how it looks?" Ellen Denning gazed at her daughter. "We have opposite styles, Cassie. You're the watcher, the listener, easy to be with, like your dad. It's why I love him. It's what people like about you too. I'm that Whirlwind Ellie who runs too fast for most people."

"You're not that bad." A thought occurred to Cassie, and she said it slowly. "You know, whenever I'm scared, or things seem too tough, I do what I think you would do — and it turns out all right."

"Really?"

"Don't spread that around."

Her mother almost smiled. Then her silent tears began again. "Oh, Cassie. No matter how much I organize and study, no matter how carefully I work, I still fail. That little boy is dead."

"Mother . . . don't beat yourself up so much. A lot of people are alive today because of you. You do more than most, but you can't do everything. It's too hard on you — and us."

Cassie's mother finished her milk slowly. Then she stood up. "There's one thing I must do though. It's been worrying me terribly. I need to find out what's troubling you. I've found an excellent doctor to help us. Will you give him a chance?"

Cassie wanted to say she wouldn't need him, she knew what was wrong. But it was late, and they'd both been through enough tonight. Instead she agreed. "Okay, Mother. I'll try — but first, tomorrow morning, you and I need to have a long talk."

Her mother nodded. "I'm sorry I've been so harsh lately. It's just that I don't want you hurt. Cassie . . . I love you."

Carefully, awkwardly, she reached for her

daughter and they held each other in the cold gloom of the first November dawn. By the time they headed upstairs to bed, beams of morning sunlight fought to push away the cold mist over Lake Erie.

The girls slept in Saturday. They woke up late, and still tired, to a dreary foggy morning.

"Cassie, I have to run," said Maya. "My uncle will be here in twenty minutes. I promised to work in the drugstore today." She rushed to the washroom.

Minutes later Cassie sat at the edge of her bed as Maya dressed. "Maya," she said. "I've been thinking. What if Catherine died really suddenly? Alone."

"What?" Maya stood still. "You mean she died, and no one knows when or how or even where her body is? That sort of thing?" Cassie nodded. "I wonder . . . That would explain why she still wanders around. She can't rest until someone finds her body and buries it."

Cassie told Maya what she had figured out, until the doorbell interrupted her.

"I've got to go. My uncle can't leave the drugstore for very long. Call you later." Maya rushed out the door saying, "I'll come back tonight. We'll talk more about this then."

Cassie followed her friend out to the car. "Hurry back. Now that I finally have some answers, I want to find out more."

"No! Wait for me. We'll call Ben, Dorian, anyone

you want. Just don't do anything alone."

"Don't worry. I'll just finish reading the ghost books you lent me. Bye . . . and thanks." She reached for Maya and hugged her.

"See you as soon as I can, Cassie. Stay safe."

Maya's uncle slid across to the passenger side, and beckoned her over to the driver's seat. She grinned at him and climbed in. She waved at Cassie, and with a jerky start headed the car down the driveway.

Cassie watched her wistfully, wishing her headaches and fatigue had not kept her from making progress on her own driving — and everything else in her life. She headed back to her room to find the books. She needed to plan.

Becky arrived home soon after, traces of Halloween make-up still on her face. "Hi, Cassie. Where's Mother?"

Cassie walked Becky to her room and told her about the accident. "The longer she sleeps today the better. She was really shaken up last night."

"Poor Mother. And that poor family." Becky shook her head sadly. Then she stopped and sniffed. "Did someone put air freshener in my room or something?"

Cassie stiffened. "No. Why?"

"I thought I smelled roses."

The picture of Catherine's hollow eyes and bony fingers examining her young sister's room struck Cassie with a bolt of pain. She gave Becky a fierce hug and walked quickly to her room to hide her tears. Becky stared after her in surprise.

When she had recovered, Cassie stood at her window overlooking the lake. It was so miserable and misty she could hardly see anything but the whitecaps churning across the sullen grey water.

Catherine, wherever you are out there, she promised herself, *you are not getting my sister . . . and you won't get me.* Unconsciously, she curled her hands into fists. She had promised to wait for Maya and the others. How ironic. First they kept bugging her to take action, now they wanted her to wait.

Cassie reached for one of Maya's ghost books. But none of them interested her now. At the bottom of the pile was the forgotten *First Families of Port Morden*. She leafed through the section on the Dennings, hoping to find something about Catherine that she'd missed. On page seventeen she noticed a line drawing of Greystones. It was an expansive view, including the lawns on the cliff and the boathouse on the beach below, with a staircase of flagstones winding between them. The caption read "Greystones, circa 1895." 1895. Catherine would have been . . . sixteen, then. She would have run across these lawns, run down that staircase on the nights she escaped to meet her "beaux" on the beach. It was gone now, probably wrecked, or buried long ago by one of the minor landslides that rolled down the cliffside from time to time.

Cassie tossed the book onto her bed and paced

her room. She felt restless, more energetic than she had in weeks. What had Maya said just before the home circle? "One of us will turn out to be the stronger one." That was me, she thought with surprise. Not efficient Maya, who I always run to for answers, not whiz kid Ben, not Dorian, hero of the school — me. I was the strongest person in that room.

Then I'm strong enough to do something — now, before the headaches and weakness return. She looked out at the stormy morning. She had to get outside, walk around, do something, before she went crazy.

She grabbed a windbreaker. It was time do what Catherine liked to do — escape. She'd try and trace Catherine's path. Maybe by following her footsteps to the beach, Cassie could find some clue about the fateful, final time Catherine had run that way.

At her door, Cassie stopped and turned back. Was she being stupid? Should she wait for her friends to help her? Should she protect herself now in some way?

But against what? She was only going out to think, to look around. She'd stop before anything dangerous could happen.

Suddenly she went to her bed and reached under her pillow. It was still there — Diana's golden locket, the one Catherine had thrown into the garbage with disgust. Without knowing why, she slipped it around her neck, ran back downstairs and out into the mist.

CHAPTER 19

The clouds hovered grey and foreboding, and the wind drove cold needles of rain at her. Cassie touched Diana's locket against her skin, and hoped what she was doing was right.

Her footprints in the grey wet grass followed her toward the cliff. Through the misty drizzle she could just see the top wooden railing of the stairway.

"Isn't it too miserable to be out walking?"

Cassie almost jumped, then turned around. Her mother stood at the back door, cool in precision-pressed jeans and shirt. Only a shadow under her eyes betrayed her earlier vulnerability. Cassie remembered their talk last night, and that was enough.

"I want to clear my head a bit. Then I have some things to tell you," she answered. "Back in a minute." She almost ran down the lawn.

From the edge, the cliff always looked higher

and steeper, the rocks below sharper. Cassie could barely see down to the beach through the mist, but she heard the waves slapping the rocks. When Catherine had run down here at night, had she followed the sound of those same waves?

Cassie explored farther along the top of the cliff. About a hundred metres along, two clumps of lilac bushes grew wild and thick. She remembered hiding in the space between them as a child, and pretending it was a pirate lookout post. The flat stone floor in it had made a handy platform for her telescope.

She pushed her way through the bushes. Did they guard the original stone path that twisted down to the beach? She kneeled down and ripped out some of the grass, until she discovered what she hoped to find. Large flat rocks. They could be the beginning of the path down — Catherine's path.

Cassie's heart pounded until she could barely breathe. She looked back. Through the drizzle and fog, she could no longer see the house, only three pale squares of light where some windows must be.

Swathed in fog and bushes, Cassie felt the dead quiet of the morning. Nothing moved in this weather. Even the lake sounded muffled from here. She wanted to race back to those squares of light, but she knew she'd never be this brave again.

One step wasn't enough. She had to make sure. If this was the stairway, she'd come back with the others later. She took a deep breath, and stepped down.

Her foot touched something solid, and slippery with damp and moss. Another stone. Good. Vines and branches twisted around and over it like greedy fingers. She lifted her foot again, and looked down. The fog shrouded the beach below so it looked like she was descending into nothing.

She put her foot down, and felt it slide. Just in time she pulled back to steady herself. It wasn't smart to grab the bushes beside her for balance, because poison ivy flourished in the dense undergrowth all over the hill.

Catherine must have been pretty desperate for fun to have climbed down here, at night and wearing a long dress, Cassie thought. Even if she didn't try it in weather like this. The fog made everything wet and slippery. It was oppressive, too. Suddenly Cassie felt her exhaustion return, along with a blazing headache. It was time to go.

Before she could turn to climb back up, a powerful push from behind surprised her. She felt herself falling and screamed, then twisted herself to the left, away from the cliff and into the bushes. She looked around wildly. No one was there.

Only a smell. Roses! Not sweet, but foul, like flowers long rotten in a vase.

Catherine!

Cassie clutched at branches as something cold and wet slapped at her face. She dared not brush it away. She needed both hands to hang on and pull herself back up the hill.

It was impossible. This was like one of those nightmares where you run and run but never move. Cassie pulled with all her strength until she felt the bush begin to give way. As it came out by the roots, she grabbed a vine and sat down, poison ivy forgotten.

Think! What do I do now? Cassie's brain was frozen with fear. She heard wailing, but she knew it wasn't her. Something strong and putrid scratched at her, forcing her to let go of the vines. She would not leave this cliff alive.

Then she appeared, a face, a shape: Catherine, pale but splendid in a shimmering gown, still ready to dance after a century of waiting. Instinctively Cassie lashed out to defend herself, and to her horror her hand hit something almost solid. Catherine sneered at Cassie and faded again into the mist.

"No!" Cassie screamed into the wind. "You're dead, Catherine. Don't you realize? You're dead!" Hanging on to anything available, she rolled into a sitting position and began to slide, around a curve, down the steep stone path.

A blow to her chest knocked the wind from her. Cassie rested and slid on. Cold slimy weeds slapped into her eyes. Not daring to brush them off with her hands, she ducked her head into her shoulder, and wiped off enough to see. Again Catherine shimmered before her, beautiful, but foul with the odour of mould and death.

Cassie panicked. She didn't want to die. Then Catherine would win, and this would all be for nothing. The thought flashed through Cassie's mind just before a rock came rolling down at her, fast, toward her head. She dodged to the left just in time. It grazed her shoulder and plunged on down into the mist.

Cassie saw where she now was, and nearly fainted. The path curved sharply to the right here. She hovered on the thin edge to nothing. The drop was hard and steep. Not even a shrub had been able to find a hold. Below her she heard the rock land with a thud against solid stone. Stone? The boat-house foundation! If she landed on that she'd be killed . . .

Another screech and a slap brought Cassie back to the present. She clawed herself away from the rocky edge, back to the vines, gasping for breath. She couldn't go on. Should she just sit here and hold on until someone missed her, until help came? She might never last through this terror that long.

"Help!" It seemed useless to shout, but maybe someone from the house would hear — if they had a window open in this weather. "Help me!"

From somewhere far out in the fog, she heard a faint answer. "Cassie, where are you? We're coming."

Had she really heard it, or was she hallucinating? It sounded like Dorian.

The vines gave a little, then more.

"Dorian. Over here. Hurry!"

"We're coming. Hang on, Cassie." This time the voice was Ben's.

She knew they couldn't make it on time. They didn't know where she was, and they were too far away in the fog. How ironic they could hear each other. On a clear day they might have seen each other, but now she might as well be alone.

Alone? A shrieking, slashing blast pushed at her, clammy and cold and reeking of rot. An avalanche of stones clattered down at her from above. Brambles scratched and tore at her. A larger rock hit the back of her head with such force she let go of the branch. With painful speed she slid and bumped down the steps, as helplessly as the debris that rolled with her. Was this how Catherine had died, slipping and falling down these steps?

Don't pass out now, she commanded herself. Stay awake. By sheer willpower, Cassie stayed conscious. She finally stopped rolling. Though her head and ankle throbbed and something damp clutched at her, she glanced around. The large dark shape of the boathouse loomed above her. She had reached the bottom.

The furious phantom pushed her again, but it didn't matter. She could no longer fall down those stairs to her death. And there was something she had to do. She brushed herself off, stood up, and limped painfully toward the boathouse.

Now the cold, shimmering figure of Catherine was in front of her, trying to push her back. She was deadly strong.

Cassie fell backward. She didn't care. She'd crawl to the boathouse if she had to. For the more Catherine pushed, the more certain Cassie was that the boathouse guarded a secret Catherine would kill to keep.

"Cassie. Where are you? Answer us — please." The muffled voices sounded frightened. She ignored them, turned, and crawled closer toward the pile of earth and brush behind the boathouse. Even with the invisible blows beating her, the grass and cuttings were easy to kick off the pile. The branches were harder to move.

Snarling and grinding her teeth, Catherine scratched and clawed and kicked. Cassie fought with all her strength, her body shaking with cold and shock. Grunting and gasping, pulling with hands and feet, she yanked a limb away. Chunks of earth flew off with it and exposed more brush underneath.

The ghost howled like a rabid wolf. Cassie grabbed a stick and, covering her bleeding face with her other hand, probed the branches.

A deadly pressure tightened around her throat. She struggled hard, but could not shake it off. Falling in a heap onto the pile, she rolled and thrashed until, choking, desperate for air, she could fight no longer. Her lungs burned with pain and panic. Waves of light and dark rolled before her eyes. She could not push away the thing squeezing the life from her.

In one last desperate effort, she clenched her fists and swung them out hard, to break the creature's hold. She wasn't strong enough.

Catherine's grip tightened. And then she touched the locket at Cassie's throat. The ghost shuddered.

Cassie gained the moment and the strength for one last try. She inhaled quickly and grabbed for a branch to use as a weapon. Nothing! She reached deeper into the pile of earth, grabbing at anything that felt solid. Finally she felt something thin and hard.

It was brittle, almost white — a skeletal hand, then an arm, crusted over with greyish patches. The remains of Catherine's glorious gown! It was — this was — Catherine's body! Free now of the brush, it lay in a twisted heap, exposed to the air it had not known for a hundred years.

With a hideous sob, the ghost of Catherine Denning loosened its deathly grip.

"Look. That's you, Catherine — dead. You're dead!" Cassie croaked the words in agony. "Now go away."

The ghost began to wail, a high-pitched sound that seemed to come from everywhere. Slowly it descended into a sob of mourning and stopped.

Cassie fainted and the beach lay silent.

CHAPTER 20

She woke up looking once again into the blue eyes of Dorian Gzowski . . . and Ben Jones worrying beside him.

"This is a habit you'll have to break, Cassie. It's tough on the nerves." Dorian smiled down at her with relief.

"Nice timing, guys," she murmured painfully, trying to reach for them. She needed to touch something warm and alive. "I did all the dirty work, and now the princes come to the rescue."

She didn't even try to get up as Ben took off his coat and wrapped it around her. She smiled at them, curled up into Ben's jacket in Dorian's arms, and let herself slide back into unconsciousness.

Weeks of rest and care healed Cassie's physical wounds, but sudden cold drafts still made her shake in fear. Talking about the ordeal with her three friends helped. They understood at least some of the horror she had survived.

"So how did you know where to find Catherine's body?" Maya had wondered.

"It was that rock that hit the boathouse. I figured that in her hurry that night, Catherine could have slipped at the curve, fallen straight down and landed in the same place. Then when her ghost tried so hard to keep me away from there, I realized it was she who kept Rumble and I away that night on the beach too. I knew that had to be it."

"It's always been creepy down there," Ben added.

Cassie shuddered. "It's awful. No one could have seen her there, either from the beach or from above. The landslide that covered half the stairs must have hit her too, and then with all the years of cuttings and stuff that people threw over the edge . . . her body was completely hidden."

"Thank God it didn't happen to you too," said Maya.

Cassie smiled at her friends. "Thank you for rescuing me," she said. It had been an anxious phone call from Maya that had sent Dorian and Ben to her rescue. They'd taken the wrong stairway and come too late, but they had come.

And her mother had shown the way. Cassie was just beginning to realize how much that had meant to her.

When she felt better, Cassie explained the whole

story to her family. They took it as well as she'd hoped they would. After all, they'd had proof — Catherine's skeleton — and some time to absorb it. Soon after, she was happy to notice the newly framed photograph of Diana in her father's office. The lost sad look on his face when her name was mentioned, had gone at last. And when Christmas came, it was the happiest one Cassie had ever had.

Catherine was finally buried properly, to rest beside her family in the cemetery above the lake. Cassie herself wrote Catherine's date of death neatly into the family Bible. Catherine would never bother a Denning daughter again.

Only her portrait remained. That saucy beautiful face still teased the world, oblivious to the tragedies it had caused. Luckily, Dan couldn't resist it after he saw it at Christmas. He took it back with him to hang in the university pub. There Catherine was finally in the centre of all the parties and dancing she could ever have wished for.

"She's gone," Maya would remind Cassie, whenever she looked sad or nervous. "Your life is normal again."

"But she's taught you something," she couldn't resist adding one evening as they sat browsing through western ranch brochures, waiting for their hair dye — item number four on Cassie's list — to take effect. "Both Dorian and Ben follow you around like puppies."

"I see you're studying a lot with that tall guy in

the science club." Cassie grinned.

Maya smiled happily. "Don't change the subject. They're waiting for you to decide which one you'll choose."

Cassie checked a damp strand of her hair, wondering how it would turn out. "I'm still sixteen. There's lots of time to choose." It felt good to be able to say that again.

"And besides," she opened a brochure wide to a page of horses and riders galloping across mountain trails, "I have a long list of things to enjoy doing first."